ROY ROGERS

and the

Gopher Creek Gunman

An original story featuring
ROY ROGERS
famous motion picture star as the hero

By
DON MIDDLETON

Illustrated by
ERWIN L. HESS

Authorized Edition

✛

WHITMAN PUBLISHING COMPANY
Racine, Wisconsin

CONTENTS

ILLUSTRATIONS

Roy Rogers Rode Through Moonlit Silence

ROY ROGERS
and the Gopher Creek Gunman

CHAPTER ONE

NIGHT FOR A MURDER

Silence, intense and oppressive, gripped the moonlit expanse of plain. The slight mist that rose from the ground gave vague and uncertain outlines to the rocks that studded the terrain like stolid sentinels. There was no breeze—no sound or motion of any sort to mar the perfect stillness. No sound, that is, except the steady clump of hoofs as a solitary rider moved through the night.

The rider was young, bronzed Roy Rogers. He sat easily in the saddle, but the muscles of his tall body were tensed and his eyes warily alert. He couldn't shake off an eerie feeling of impending trouble. Neither could he account for that strange anxiety.

The golden palomino seemed to share his rider's disquiet. Trigger trotted smoothly and swiftly through the night, but his ears were twin points and his nostrils quivered.

"What's got into us, Trigger?" Roy asked in a low

11

voice as he leaned forward to pat the horse's neck. "We're as nervy as a couple of colts. Everything certainly *looks* peaceful. There's not a living critter in sight anywhere."

It was the first time Roy had ever felt this uneasiness. He had traveled countless miles in the dark of night, with only Trigger and the stars for companions. Because he had spent half his life in the saddle, complete solitude and trackless country were nothing new to him.

Roy had been a cowboy for as long as he could remember. He loved the wild, free life of the plains. He had tamed broncs, hazed cattle, ridden point on trail drives, bulldogged the toughest of steers and won a dozen rodeo championships.

He knew the mountains and plains in all kinds of weather. He was familiar with every detail of the country through which he traveled. He could identify the call of every creature of the West and he knew the name of every tree and shrub. He was completely at home in the moonlit silence of the night.

There was no explanation for the feeling of depression that had fallen over him like a shroud. He hadn't felt that way at sunset. What was there about the darkness of this particular night that disturbed him?

Roy was heading for country where oil had recently been discovered. A week before he had run into an old prospector, just in from the oil fields. As he listened to the old man's stories of the excitement of prospecting for oil, the suspense of drilling down through the sun-baked earth, and the thrill of watching the stream of "black gold" gush upward toward the sky, Roy had decided to take a look at this new world of derricks and machines and grim-faced men.

Now, as he rode toward the oil fields, Roy Rogers was on the way to greater excitement and adventure than he had ever known.

He started to whistle, but the tune quickly died away.

"Hang it all," he muttered. "I can't shake this mood. I guess I've been in the saddle too long. It's about time to pitch camp and turn in."

Ahead loomed a clump of trees, silhouetted as a patch of black against the sky. Though it was early evening, the rider decided to camp somewhere among those trees. As Trigger brought him near the wooded area, Roy heard the sound of running water. Trigger's ears cocked forward at the rippling sound and Roy grinned in the darkness.

"That's all you need to hear, eh, Trigger? I can let the reins fall and you'll head for that stream," he said to the palomino.

Cool leaves of low branches brushed Roy's face and the broad, slightly curled-up brim of his high-crowned hat. Then Trigger stopped abruptly, his strong muscles quivering. Roy glanced sharply ahead and gasped in surprise as his eyes met those of another man on a level with his own. The moonlight, slanting through an opening in the trees, fell full upon the other man's face. For a moment Roy Rogers could only stare in disbelief. Then he realized that the man in front of him was dead, suspended from the branches overhead by a noose about his neck. His feet dangled several inches off the ground.

Roy nudged Trigger ahead until he reached the dead man. Then, supporting the stranger with an arm about the waist, he whipped out his sheath knife and cut the rope, lowering the unconscious form to the ground as he dismounted.

Roy's hands trembled slightly as he fumbled in the saddle bag for an electric torch. Though calm in the face of danger and at home in the excitement of competition, Roy, like most men, was awed by death.

He found his flashlight and spilled white light over the still figure on the ground. He saw the face of a man about his own age, a face tanned by good, clean sunshine, with freckles to match the sandy hair. Though not a handsome face, it was the face of a man one would like to know.

The light fell on a note pinned to the pocket of

the dead man's faded, but clean, blue denim shirt. Roy Rogers moved a little closer to read the words crudely formed on a grubby sheet of paper apparently torn from a notebook.

The note said: "This is to worn all concerned that they gotta clear off of land that ayent there own. Keep off of the oil fields or you will get the same." The message, with its misspelled words, was signed "Indian Pete."

Roy was careful to preserve whatever fingerprints there might be on the note. He drew out the pin, then used it to lift the note from the dead man's chest to his own pocket handkerchief. This he folded carefully and tucked into his wallet.

"I don't know Indian Pete," he muttered, "but it's a pretty safe bet that he's not the one who did this. He'd hardly sign his name to murder."

He scrutinized the dead man with more attention to detail. A large bump on the back of the young fellow's head indicated that he might have been slugged into unconsciousness before being hanged.

Nothing indicated that a struggle had preceded the hanging. The dead man's face showed no bruises, and his hands were clean, the knuckles unmarked. The blue shirt and dark trousers were neat and clean, though well worn, and the shoes were polished.

It is a curious and undeniable fact that the mere

finding of a dead or injured person entails certain responsibilities. It was out of the question for Roy to tell himself that this was none of his affair, and so ride away. The thought of doing so never entered his head. He searched the dead man's pockets for a clue to his identity, but found nothing. Someone, doubtless the murderer, had cleaned them out.

Roy splashed the light on the ground but found no sign of hoof or boot marks. He realized, when he examined his own backtrail, that the sun-baked earth was too hard to register a trail. There was no way to learn the direction from which the murdered man had come or where he had been going. There was nothing to show whether he had been on foot or horseback, or the number of men who had attacked him.

Roy switched off the flashlight while he pondered. It was, he knew, a full day's ride to the nearest town, still longer if Trigger had to carry a double burden. He considered the idea of leaving things as they were while he rode alone for officials of the law. One day going and another day coming would mean that the hangman's victim would lie for at least two days. Roy shuddered at the thought of what prairie wolves and buzzards would do in the meantime.

He didn't waste much time in meditation, but quickly considered and rejected the various possibilities before he decided to unpack his spade and bury the young man. He didn't consider the legal aspects of such a move, but only that it was the simple, logical thing to do.

He unbuckled the straps that held his soogan in place behind the saddle, opened the roll and selected the heavier of two blankets. Spreading this on the ground, he wrapped the dead man carefully and then turned to his spade.

Though the night was well advanced when Roy finished, he abandoned his original intention to make camp. After a refreshing dip in the cool, swift-running stream, he dressed and made up his blanket roll, strapping it behind the saddle.

"We're shoving on, Trigger," he told his horse. "I'm going to see what we can learn about the gent called Indian Pete."

CHAPTER TWO

ATTACK

It was one of those heavy, oppressive nights that strain the nerves of man and beast. The one-eyed, grizzled old man paced like a caged beast, back and forth within the narrow confines of a small shack beneath an oil derrick. He growled and muttered as he paced. He complained about the uncertainties of oil drilling, and about the weather. He grumbled about his aches and pains, and he beefed about the world in general. His name was Lonergan, but everyone who knew him called him "Gimlet."

Gimlet Lonergan had spent more years than he could count in a hopeless pursuit of fortune. He had helped drill for oil in many parts of the country. Perhaps it was these years of boring into Mother Earth which had inspired his nickname, but a far more likely explanation might be found in the penetrating way he had of glaring with his one piercing eye.

Gimlet was small, lean and wiry. That part of his face not covered with a stubby, bristly, snow-white beard was wrinkled and weathered like the skin of an old chestnut. Yet, despite his indeterminate age, the old man was hard as nails. As he paced, his

18

wrath crystallized into two chief complaints, the first of which dealt with a half-breed known as Indian Pete.

"Just imagine the brass-bound nerve of that mangy coyote," Gimlet sputtered. "Where in the name of a triple-twisted tornado does he get the idea that *he* owns this land?"

Dick Collins didn't answer, because the question didn't seem to call for an answer. He simply grinned at his old partner's ire, and stretched his long legs out on the bunk on which he sat.

"Take it easy, Gimlet," he said easily. "It won't help any to get yourself riled up."

"It ain't only the thoughts of that buzzard-faced breed that rile me," spouted Gimlet. "It's the way your kid brother is stayin' away so doggoned long." He spat through an open window, turned, and strode across the room once more.

"You're just borrowing trouble when you worry about Tom."

"Tom should be back!"

"He'll be back as soon as he can make it. It's quite a ride over to the ranch."

"He shouldn't never o' gone at all in the first place. What right's he got to sashay off to visit his girl an' her family when we're in danger of bein' called on by Indian Pete an' his no-account friends?"

"If Indian Pete comes here, we'll take care of

him," promised Dick.

Gimlet halted and settled his gaze on Dick's mild, bronzed face. "Fer a redhead," he said, "it shore takes you a long time tuh git fightin' mad."

"I can get fighting mad when it'll do some good, but right now the only thing we can do is wait. What's more, Gimlet, we can turn in and get a night's sleep. Time won't pass any faster because we stay awake to watch it."

"*Sleep!*" exploded Gimlet. "Humph!" He started pacing again. After two lengths of the room he halted and spoke.

"Dick."

"Yes, Gimlet."

"Are you dead sure that Indian Pete ain't got no legal claim tuh this yere piece of land we're drillin'?"

"Of course I'm sure of it. I checked up on the title to the land before we made a deal to buy it. The owner is the man from whom we bought the option, Lem Bixby."

"You ain't got no doubt about that?"

Dick Collins shook his head slowly and said, "None."

"Then maybe I'm just wastin' my time with worryin' about Indian Pete."

"Of course, you are."

"All right then, Dick," went on the old fellow, "p'raps you c'n relieve me of one more worry. D'you

Gimlet Halted in His Pacing

think we'll strike oil before the option expires?"

"I hope so."

"But you ain't sure?"

"No one can be sure of anything where oil drilling's concerned. You know that as well as I do, Gimlet."

"But you *think* we'll strike oil before the option runs out, don't yuh, Dick?" Gimlet seemed desperately anxious, and eager for reassurance.

"I think we will, Gimlet. As soon as we strike the oil, Abe Geesel will put up enough cash for us to buy the land outright by taking up our option."

"Thar's another worry that's ranklin' my soul."

"What's that, Gimlet?"

"Abe Geesel. I shore wish we hadn't o' had tuh let that crook in on our plans."

"Why do you call Geesel a crook?"

"Because he's in the moneylendin' business, an' he's got a shifty look about him. I don't like him."

Dick Collins laughed. "You don't like him, so he must be a crook, is that it, Gimlet?"

Gimlet didn't reply.

"Let's not worry about Geesel," Dick continued. "He's promised to put up the cash to buy this land as soon as we hit the oil. We've got his promise in writing, so we needn't think about him."

Gimlet thought it over while he paced the room. He paused and looked through the window, into the night. Dick Collins knew what was coming next.

"Wonder where Tom is."

"So you've gone back to worrying about Tom!"

"Um."

"Why don't you go to bed, Gimlet? I'll stay up and let you know when Tom returns."

"We shouldn't o' let him go to that ranch alone, Dick, not with all the threats that Indian Pete's been makin'."

"Tom wanted to go and it would have taken horses to hold him back."

"Humph," snorted Gimlet.

"You've got to make allowances for a young fellow in love."

"Love! Humph! There's plenty of time fer that tomfoolery when we get tuh the oil. Tom knows darn well that we're workin' against time."

"We'll get the oil before the option runs out, Gimlet. You'll see. We'll torpedo the shaft tomorrow or next day and then the old pay stuff will shoot up. See if I'm not right."

As far as Dick was concerned, the matter was closed. He paid no further attention to Gimlet's growled complaints. The old man seemed to feel personally offended at Tom's failure to return on schedule. He muttered complaints about the unfair treatment he and Dick were being given, he cussed the luck which kept them on this job so long without success, and he tossed off a few blistering remarks about girls who "kept a man from honest work." Through it all he was in ceaseless motion, stalking around the small room, moving a chair six inches to the side, adjusting pots and pans and skillets on the stove, rearranging cans and boxes on a shelf. From time to time he glanced at Dick and snorted at a picture of perfect relaxation.

Dick lay back on the bunk with his hands clasped behind his head. His eyes were open, but held a faraway look that told Gimlet he was quite unaware of the old man's presence.

Dick was thinking of the day six months ago when he and Tom had come into the west. He remembered their visit to the ranch of a friend named Bart Hastings, who owned the Bar H outfit a day and a half to the west. It was, in fact, Bart Hastings who had suggested that they try their hand at oil.

Dick thought of the day he and Tom had found old Gimlet Lonergan, more nearly dead than alive after a spill into a ravine. They had patched the old man up and taken care of him until he was able to take care of himself. By that time they had grown really fond of the fiery old fellow and a partnership had come about in the natural course of events.

Gimlet had knocked around that country for the greater part of his life, and he knew oil land when he saw it. Best of all, he knew the practical side of oil drilling. His knowledge had come from hard years of working for oil drillers, whereas Dick and Tom had gleaned their knowledge from books.

Hastings had told about a piece of land which might be worth investigating. When Gimlet saw the land, his enthusiasm had bubbled over. He had declared stoutly that he'd stake his reputation, which meant little, and his life, which meant a lot, on the fact that there was oil a-plenty beneath the surface.

Dick's eyes lost their distant expression and his mind returned to the present when he thought he heard a faint sound outside the shack. Tense, he strained his ears to catch the sound. He glanced at Gimlet and saw the old fellow smoking his pipe as he sat with his one eye riveted on the door. There was no repetition of the sound.

Dick returned to his reverie. He remembered how he had gone to the owner of the land, a man named Lem Bixby, with the pooled cash of his brother and himself. Because it hadn't been enough to buy the land outright, Dick had made the best deal he could. He had bought an option on the land, then found himself in the unpleasant position of owning oil land with no cash to go after the oil. That was when he had gone to Abe Geesel.

He hadn't liked Abe Geesel, but personal liking meant nothing in matters of hard cash. Geesel, a man of affairs in the town of Gopher Creek, had drawn up an agreement whereby he would finance the drilling of the land for a share in the oil, if and when it was brought to the surface.

Dick yawned and stretched luxuriously. There was every indication that oil would be found within the next few days, or a week at most. Then there would be easy sailing ahead.

He had discounted all the petty rumblings of a dissolute character called Indian Pete. He thought nothing about them.

Gimlet tapped out the ashes, stuck his stubby pipe in the pocket of his unbuttoned vest, rose and looked at Dick. The older brother was grinning.

"I reckon," the old man said in a milder tone than he had used before, "I'm nothin' but an old fool. But I can't help worryin'. It just seems that somethin' is dead sure to happen before the oil comes in. It just don't seem natural fer me tuh have any good luck that'd put more'n two bits of cash intuh my pockets."

"You'll have two-bit pieces to throw to chickens in another couple of months," promised Dick.

Then it began.

The door burst open with a suddenness that jerked Dick to a sitting position. He had a quick glance at a dark-skinned face beyond the barrel of a leveled six-gun before the gun spat smoke and fire with a roar that fairly rocked the flimsy building. Dick felt the rush of a slug fan his cheek and heard the thud as the bullet drilled the wood of the wall behind him.

A roar of dismay and surprise came from Gimlet. Dick heard that bellow as he leaped. He tore himself from the bunk, diving headfirst toward the intruder. His shoulder caught the gunman at the knees and both men crashed to the floor in a tangle of waving arms and legs.

There they struggled, each trying to get a grip on the other. Dick heard confusion above him, but his energies were concentrated on the man with whom he fought. He wasn't aware of the three other men who rushed through the open door. He saw nothing but the greasy, livid face mere inches from his own, and heard only snarls and threats against a vague background of confusion. Gimlet's voice, shrieking in rage, was part of a wild surge of noise. Then one of the intruders raised a gun, to bring the barrel down on Dick's unprotected head with stunning force. Dick saw a million brilliant lights, then nothing.

Gimlet let out a howl of rage. Snatching his own gun from a holster on the chair, he fired point-blank into the knot of men near the door. One of them screamed as the lead grazed his cheek.

"Blast yuh!" yelled the old man. "Hyar's some more!" But before he could fire, two men slammed him back against the bunk.

"Take 'em alive!" shrilled a voice above the clamor. "We want to string 'em up as a warnin' to others."

Rough hands tried to throttle Gimlet. The squirming old man seemed possessed of superhuman strength as he fought off attempts to rope him.

Dick thought he was having a nightmare in which a dark-skinned, pock-marked face with ugly, leering eyes and yellowed fang-like teeth filled the screen of his vision. A roaring, whirring sound seemed to fill his brain to bursting before the roaring resolved itself into shouted cries and yells and scuffling feet. The nightmarish face was a reality, the loathsome features really above him.

Dick was flat on his back on the floor of the cabin. A man sat astride his chest, trying to capture his arms to tie them. Dick had apparently been fighting, even though his mind had momentarily gone blank.

Conscious now, Dick Collins threw all of his strength into one mighty effort. He jerked one arm free of the hand that clutched it, balled his fist, and swung as best he could from his awkward position. He felt a jar as his fist connected, and saw the halfbreed reel to one side. He rolled quickly, following up the advantage of the blow, and squirmed out from beneath the pock-marked man.

Then he was on his feet with the agility of a panther. He swung at the nearest man and had the satisfaction of seeing him stagger back against the table.

The table went down and the oil lamp went with it. As the glass reservoir smashed into thousands of tiny pieces a quart of coal oil splashed over the floor. For a moment the room was dark. Then, as the five-foot puddle of oil picked up the flare of the wick, flames rose to light the scene with flickering, uneven gleams. The fire spread quickly and licked greedily at the bone-dry wood of the shack.

Gimlet was on the floor, flat on his back, his arms and legs waving and kicking furiously against the efforts of two men to hold him down. Dick lowered his head and charged. He struck the two with a force that sent them sprawling. Following up his advantage, the redhead jabbed one man in the stomach and lashed out with his fist against the chin of the other. He had the satisfaction of knowing from startled grunts that both blows were effective, but he didn't pause to see *how* effective they were. Whirling, he grabbed a handful of Gimlet's shirt and jerked the old man to his feet.

"Lemme at 'em!" bellowed Gimlet. "Lemme git a crack at them buzzards!"

"Get out of here!" cried Dick.

"We gotta finish 'em off!"

"The fire will finish *us*, if we don't get out!"

Dick shoved Gimlet ahead of him in the general direction of the door. Once started, Gimlet kept going.

Dick paused to glance behind him. One entire wall of the shack was ablaze and the flames were licking at the roof. The air was fast becoming unbearable. Dick saw that the four attackers were on their feet and able to leave the raging inferno without his help. Then he dashed into the open.

Gimlet stood ten paces from the shack, his fists balled and waving in bloodthirsty gestures of defiance.

"Lemme at 'em!" he yelled. "All I want is the chance tuh meet 'em in the open."

"We'd better get away from here," said Dick, shouting to make himself heard above the roaring, crackling flames.

"We ain't finished the fight!"

"We can finish it some other time. There're four of them and two of us!"

"There may be fourteen of 'em the next time! What's the matter with you, Collins? Can't you handle two of those rats?"

"Listen to me, you crazy galoot," began Dick.

"I ain't leavin' here! If you want tuh clear out I'll try tuh handle all four of 'em!"

"Crazy fool!"

"They started this fight an', by Juniper, I aim tuh finish it!"

There was no time for further argument. The enemy burst from the shack and rushed at Dick and Gimlet.

CHAPTER THREE

TRIGGER TO THE RESCUE

Roy Rogers was in the saddle with his soogan tied behind, but he wasn't quite ready to set out on the man hunt. There was one detail remaining.

Gripping the flashlight beneath his left arm, Roy drew his gun, opened it, and dumped the cartridges into the palm of his hand. He snapped the empty cylinder back in place and drew the trigger slowly while he studied the weapon's action with the critical eye of an expert in firearms. He drew back the hammer with his thumb, held back the trigger, then lowered the hammer carefully. Satisfied that the pistol was in perfect condition, he reloaded it and dropped it into the holster, switched out the light and stowed the torch in a saddlebag.

"Now," he muttered, "I guess we're ready to shove on. Get along, Trigger."

The palomino needed no further cue. He fairly leaped forward, but slowed quickly as a large tree loomed dead ahead.

There had been nothing to tell which way the murderers had gone. Since they might have taken one of many possible directions when they left the scene of the hanging, Roy decided to travel his original course until he found reason to change.

He let the reins fall slack, knowing that Trigger would make better time if permitted to pick his own way in and out among the trees. It took more than half an hour to traverse the woods and reach the flat, open plain.

In the open once again, Roy noted with satisfaction that the fog had disappeared. Though the night was not quite as clammy as it had been, it was still humid and sticky enough to be unpleasant.

Trigger kept to a steady lope that covered the ground with a minimum of effort. Roy set the horse's nose toward a star low in the eastern sky. The horse, he knew, would maintain the pace and direction until new cues were given by the rider.

Roy lost track of time and distance. Riding steadily forward, he remembered his days as a sheriff's deputy, when he had run down lawbreakers. All that Roy had learned in tracking and trailing came back to him now.

At first only vaguely aware of the gentle hill ahead, Roy snapped to alert attention when he saw that the crest of the hill was outlined against a red glow.

That glow was not the light of dawn. Dawn was hours away. There could be only one other explanation. Fire!

"We'd better travel!" Roy called to Trigger, as he

nudged the horse's sides.

The speed increased. Trigger's powerful muscles came into more active play as the palomino thundered up the slope. Roy heard the sound of battle. Words were indistinguishable, but the emotions of the men who cried out were unmistakable. There were shrill cries of pain, shouts of rage and fury and the rasped grunts of struggling men.

Trigger charged up the hill as if he too knew what lay beyond the crest. Roy caught the smell of burning wood a moment before he saw the fire.

Flames leaped high above the burning shack and made the skeleton-like pyramid of an oil derrick stand out in bold relief. Between the hard-riding cowboy and the flames, six men struggled furiously. Roy's quick eye and brain sized up the situation at once.

Two men fought bravely against four. The fight was hand to hand and the two were back to back. As Roy charged nearer he saw one of the two go down from a vicious blow on the head. Someone aimed a kick at his side, but the kick didn't land. The tall, broad-shouldered fellow, turning quickly, leaped in with a sharp jab that lifted the would-be kicker off his feet.

Now four men remained standing, one putting up a valiant stand against the other three. Roy chose sides instinctively as Trigger swept him to the fight.

Dick Collins knew the fight was nearly over. His vision was blurred by a red mist and his breath came in choking sobs that burned his throat. His arms were heavy as he lifted them painfully from his sides. He fought on, in a daze, but found himself wishing for oblivion. He knew Gimlet was down, unconscious, possibly dead. He found himself envying the old man. Gimlet no longer had to endure the wracking pain of countless blows and the searing burn of overtaxed lungs.

Then Dick couldn't lift his arms. Two men held them to his sides. He was helpless. His knees began to cave, but those who gripped him from the rear kept him from falling. A roaring sound filled his brain, but over it he heard a snarling voice shout cruel instructions.

"Don't let him go down! Keep him on his feet until I work him over an' teach him a lesson he won't forget."

Blows fell furiously on Dick's unprotected face, but he no longer felt them. He could hear the crash of fist on face, but there was no longer any sensation of pain. He was aware of the blows in a detached sort of way.

He heard hoofbeats, but these, too, were merely vague and meant nothing. He heard the roar of a gun. The sudden blast hammered against his brain and shook off some of the cobwebs. Dick opened his eyes as far as their swollen condition would permit. He saw the man in front of him falling back, screaming in pain and fury while he hugged a wounded wrist.

Dick didn't know, until it was explained to him later, that there had been not one but two shots fired. Roy Rogers's bullet, an infinitesimal fraction of a second ahead of the half-breed's, had unquestionably saved Dick's life.

Dick felt himself slumping to the ground. Even as he fell, he heard coarse cries and gunfire from the men who had held him. A horse reared high, and in his distorted vision it seemed that horse and rider towered miles above him.

Roy's charge had been so sudden—so unexpected—that he had arrived on the scene before the attackers were aware of him. After his quick shot at the gun-slinger's wrist, he jammed his weapon into the holster before it stopped smoking. His horse reared high, and from the peak of the rise, Rogers threw himself headlong from the saddle at the two men who tried to bring their guns to bear.

He felt bullets fan his head, and then his outflung hands found the shoulders of the men standing side by side. He shifted his grip to their necks, then brought his hands together like a musician playing cymbals. Sharp screams of pain split the air as the renegades' heads cracked together. Roy let go and dropped into a crouch. He was out of it with panther-like speed, driving his fist ahead of him in a stunning uppercut. He saw one man's head snap back, then whirled in time to duck a vicious blow as the other clubbed with the barrel of his gun. He jabbed, sinking his fist to the wrist in the stomach of the cursing outlaw.

For the first time the breed with the wounded wrist realized that defeat was not only possible, but quite likely. He saw his three companions on the ground, two totally unconscious and the third rolling in agony. Curses filled the air. The breed forgot his wounded wrist. He scooped up his gun in his left hand and leveled it at the cowboy who had so suddenly changed the tide of battle.

Roy saw the weapon. He saw the half-breed's finger squeezing the trigger and was aware of the twisted grin of conquest that distorted the gunman's pock-marked face. Time stood still in that split second. Roy couldn't duck or dodge that bullet. He couldn't get at his own gun in time to defend himself. He waited, and it seemed an eternity, for the bullet that was sure to find its mark.

Then Trigger took a hand. He rose up, then lashed down with his forehoofs. Just as the half-breed was about to fire, he was struck between the shoulders with amazing force. He was falling as he completed his trigger squeeze. The bullet plowed into the ground at Roy's feet as the half-breed fell unconscious.

It took the cowboy several minutes to recover his breath. During this time he surveyed the scene of battle. Six men lay on the ground in grotesque positions. Five of the six were unconscious, the other was still gasping for breath after Roy's blow to the stomach.

Four were half-breeds. Rogers turned to examine the two white men by the light of the burning building.

CHAPTER FOUR

The roof of the shack fell in with a shower of
sparks and flying embers. The sudden increase in
draft sent leaping tongues of flame higher than the
top of the derrick. Then the walls collapsed, and
for several minutes the flames roared with renewed
fury before they died down to a steady burning that
would continue until every stick of the structure
was consumed. By the firelight Roy Rogers began a
methodical examination of the wounded men.

He had barely begun when he realized that three
of the half-breeds were beginning to stir. Their
grunts and groans were the first symptoms of return-
ing consciousness. These men, Roy knew, were
killers. They had shown that by the cruel way in
which they had pummeled the helpless man. Roy
decided to take no chances. He would tie them up
before they became interested in renewing the fight.

He took his lariat from the saddle and measured
off a six-foot length. Then he hesitated. It was a
shame to cut up that length of line. Roy had taken
pains to make it perfect. He had selected the original rope with meticulous care, and then tested
every inch for strength and uniformity. The honda

39

had been handmade by one of his closest friends in
Mexico. Roy had spent hours working the rope to
make it soft and pliable. He glanced at the three
who stirred on the ground, then tossed the coiled
lasso over the horn of his saddle.

He turned the nearest of the half-breeds over on
his back and unfastened the buckle of his belt and
the knot of his bandanna. The belt, looped twice
about the ankles and buckled as tightly as possible,
would keep the breed from walking. Unceremo-
niously he rolled the grunting man over on his face
and brought his wrists together at the small of his
back. The bandanna would keep them there.

"That'll hold him for a while," Roy mused.

It was the work of but a few minutes to give the
same deft treatment to the others. None of the half-
breeds offered the slightest resistance.

A moment's glance told Roy that the fourth half-
breed, the one with the pock-marked face, would
need no tying. It was he who had drawn the gun
on Roy. In one of those curious twists by which Fate
sometimes seems to deal out justice, the ugly-faced
man was dead. In falling forward he had come
directly into the line of a thrown knife. The hilt of
the weapon stuck out from his left side a few inches
below the armpit. Roy realized that the man he had
jabbed in the stomach must have aimed the blade,
and the dead man had dropped into it as it flew

toward Roy, himself.

Gimlet's face was badly bruised. Roy brought out a small kit which he laid open on the ground. He touched the many small cuts and abrasions with an antiseptic lotion, then fastened pads of sterilized gauze over the worst of the cuts. The dressings looked particularly white with Gimlet's sun-browned, leathery skin as background.

The half-breeds watched his every move. Their small black eyes, reflecting the glow of the fire, bore a close resemblance to the steady gaze of a serpent trying to hypnotize a bird. The prisoners, however, were making no attempt to loosen their bonds. They seemed to accept their capture with stoic silence, as if they knew that struggle, appeal, and argument would be futile.

Roy winced at the sight of Dick Collins's face. He washed away the bloody sweat and dirt with a touch as gentle as that of a trained nurse. Dick had been battered cruelly by the man who was now dead. He had been hammered with hard, ruthless fists long after he was beyond resistance. His face was swollen until it looked bloated. There was a deep break in the skin beneath one eyebrow.

"If I had the tools," Roy muttered, examining the cut, "I'd take a couple of stitches in that so it would heal better."

Not having the necessary equipment, he fashioned what are sometimes called "adhesive stitches." He notched a piece of tape in such a way that it was narrowest where it crossed the line of broken flesh, and wide at each side of the break. This served to close the opening.

"Maybe a doctor can fix it a little better in the morning," Rogers told himself when he had finished.

Dick's lips were swollen but the skin was unbroken.

There was something about the boy's face, distorted though it was, that struck a familiar chord in Roy's mind. During the time he had been working over it, he had been trying to recall where he had seen Dick Collins previously. He seemed to see the same freckled nose, the same sandy hair that started high on the forehead, and the same square jaw. Then it came to him. He was looking at features like those of the man he had buried a few hours ago. The resemblance was unmistakable.

When Roy saw Dick's lips move slowly he poured water from his canteen onto a wad of clean cotton from the first-aid kit and held this against the tortured mouth.

Dick gave a soft groan.

"Take it easy," said Roy.

Dick's lips tried to form a word.

"Don't try to talk for a little while. You'll be all right. Just lie back there and rest."

"Take It Easy," Said Roy Soothingly

Dick's eyes opened the slightest bit. His lips moved once more.

"G-Gimlet," he whispered hoarsely.

Roy didn't understand the word, but he smiled confidently so Dick could see him, and said, "Just rest for a few minutes, then you can talk. Everything is under control."

"M-My friend, Gimlet—old man—is—is he all right?" The simple speech required a maximum of effort.

"You mean the old fellow with you?"

"Y-Yes."

"He's all right."

"Are—are you sure?"

Roy glanced toward the lean old man and observed the steady rise and fall of his chest.

"He's still unconscious," he said, "but he's breathing easily and I'm sure he'll be up and around in a little while."

Dick nodded.

"Would you like a drink of water?"

Dick indicated that he would.

Roy placed an arm beneath Dick's shoulders and lifted him far enough to sip from the canteen. "Not too much," he cautioned. "Just a swallow or two. You may have more in a few minutes."

Dick mumbled thanks and sighed as he was lowered to the ground. He closed his eyes, and for a moment Roy thought he had lapsed back into unconsciousness. Then he heard Dick mumble.

"Be all right—in—in a few minutes—," he said with frequent pauses. "I—I j-just want to rest—."

"You stay right there as long as you want. I've got to rig up some kind of a shelter and it'll take a little time."

Roy rose to his feet to consider the idea of a shelter. There was a small tool shed, but it was far too small to be used by men. A couple of horses were in a fenced-in area. The only other structure was the towering derrick.

"We've got to have a shelter of some sort," Roy muttered to Trigger. "I don't know how soon these men can travel. If they have to stay here while the sun is up they'll bake, if they're not protected."

Trigger's head moved as if he understood every word.

For the second time that evening, Roy unbuckled the straps that held his duffel in place behind the saddle. He still had one large blanket and a poncho. He also carried a large square tarpaulin that served many purposes. The tarp not only kept his blanket roll dry in rainy weather, it also served as a tent or groundcloth. Tonight, augmented by the poncho, it would shelter the injured men.

Roy fastened the tarpaulin to the base of the derrick, about five feet from the ground. He stretched it, slanting, to meet the ground, and pegged it in place. Using heavy blanket pins, he arranged the poncho on one side, then spread the blanket on the ground. With the firelight creeping in, this shelter was cosier than one might imagine.

The cowboy then carried Gimlet and Dick into the lean-to and laid them gently on the blanket. He unsaddled Trigger and haltered him near by. Then, at last, Roy himself could relax. He flopped on the blanket beside Dick Collins.

CHAPTER FIVE

RECOVERY

Dick's head throbbed painfully. The slightest movement brought new waves of giddiness that beat against his brain and threatened to deprive him of his uncertain grip on consciousness. He opened his eyes slowly, but quickly closed them as a sheet of dancing flame met his gaze blindingly. He heard crackling flames, and heard a low voice speaking somewhere near at hand, but the words were without meaning. His mind a maelstrom of worry, he lay still, trying to piece together some of the pictures whirling so vaguely through his brain. There was something about a burning building—there was a note of worry about his brother Tom—there was a fight in which he had a fleeting glimpse of a pock-marked face grinning with loathsome evil.

Then Dick realized that he lay on a blanket. He could feel the soft wool beneath his hands. He tried an experimental movement of his head and found that now he could move without the feeling of nausea that his last similar experiment had caused. He opened his eyes again and kept them open. Some kind of shelter was overhead, and now the words of the man who spoke made sense.

"I was heading this way," Roy Rogers said, "when I saw the row. You seemed to be having a rocky time of it so I dealt myself in. That is, Trigger and I did."

Dick turned toward the voice. He saw Roy grinning in a friendly sort of way.

"That's the stuff," the young cowboy said. "You're coming around all right. Just take it easy. You can't rush things, when you're coming out of a beating like you took."

The clouds in Dick's brain thinned. Roy lifted him so that he might take more water from the canteen. In a few minutes he was able to sit up, his back propped against the base of the oil derrick, and take stock of his surroundings. Though his head still throbbed, he was fully conscious. He saw Gimlet motionless at his side, but Roy quickly reassured him, promising that the old man would be all right in a little while.

"I guess there's no doubt about what you did, stranger," said Dick. "You saved our lives. Those breeds meant business."

"Trigger's the one to thank."

"Who?"

"That's my horse's name," grinned Roy. "My name's Rogers—Roy Rogers!"

"I sure don't know how to thank you for what you've done," Dick said quietly, looking at Roy with warm gratitude in his eyes. "They had us down for the count. I hate to think of what would have happened if you hadn't come along just when you did."

"Don't even try to think of it," Roy smiled. "It didn't happen, and you and the old man are goin' to be all right. What's your name?"

"I'm Dick Collins. The old man's name is Lonergan. Everybody calls him Gimlet."

"I'm glad to know you, Dick." Roy put out his hand and Dick grasped it heartily.

"I'm sure glad to know you! I'm sorry we caused you so much trouble, Mr. Rogers."

"The name's Roy."

"Thanks—er—Roy." Dick's bruised and battered face wrinkled in a grin. Then he grew soberly serious again as he looked at Roy. "I won't try to tell you how much I appreciate what you did. You sure took an awful chance, barging into a fight with those four murderin' breeds. And to help a couple of strangers, too."

"I like a good fight," Roy laughed. Embarrassed by the open admiration and gratitude in Dick's eyes and voice, he spoke quickly to turn the conversation into other channels. "I started to tell you," he said, "how Trigger saved our necks."

"Oh, yes."

"I thought one of the men I poked in the stomach was out of the fight, but he wasn't *all* the way out.

He could still throw a knife, and that's what he did."

"At you?" asked Dick with quick, excited alarm. He was amazed at the smiling calm of this tanned young cowboy who had waded without hesitation into a desperate fight between men he had never seen before. Dick shuddered, thinking how easily that thrown knife might have ended Roy's life before he even knew with whom, or for whom, he was fighting.

"Yes," Roy answered his question. "And at the same minute he threw the knife, another of the half-breeds had the drop on me. He was squeezing the trigger when my horse took a hand and slapped at his back. The killer fell forward and took the knife."

"Gosh!" Dick exclaimed. "That was a close one! Those crooks meant to murder us."

"They came mighty close to succeeding." Roy frowned, remembering the brutal cruelty of that firelit battle.

"Too close for comfort," Dick agreed.

"Are you and Gimlet partners?" Roy asked with friendly interest.

Dick nodded. "Gimlet knows a lot about oil drilling. We've been working on this land for several months now. We hope to strike oil pretty soon."

"Just the two of you?"

"No, Mr. Rog—er—Roy." Dick laughed a little, and then went on. "It's a four-way proposition. My brother Tom is with us. The fourth is the man who put up some cash."

Roy tensed at the mention of a brother. He remembered, all too clearly, the man he'd buried, the one who looked so much like Dick. He found it hard to make his next question casual. "Where's your brother?"

"He's been away from here for a few days. He has a girl over at the Rockin' Jay ranch. He rode over to see her and her folks."

"I see."

A shadow of worry crossed Dick's face. "He should've been back by this time. I hope nothing's happened to him."

Roy knew that Dick was in for a crushing piece of news. He wanted to postpone that news a little longer. Dick would need all of his courage to take the blow. "What about the fourth man?" he asked. "The one who put up cash."

Dick then explained how he and Tom had teamed up with Gimlet and how the three had spent their cash for the option on the land. "Then we got working capital from Abe Geesel. He's in business in Gopher Creek."

"What kind of a deal have you with him?" Roy wanted to keep Dick talking.

"If we don't strike oil before the option runs out, everything is off."

"In that case you don't have to repay the loan?"

"No. But, of course, we'd lose all we paid for the option as well as all the work we've put in on this job."

"What happens if you strike oil?"

"In that case, Geesel will put up the cash to buy the land by taking up the option. We'll split everything four ways and the three of us will repay Geesel the cash he advanced."

"Then Geesel's in for a quarter interest."

"That's right."

"Dick, why did those four half-breeds come here?"

"I forgot all about them!" exclaimed Dick, trying to rise. He slumped back to the blanket with a slight moan of futility.

"You're not ready to get up just yet, Dick. Take it easy for a little while."

"I—I'm weaker than I thought."

"Of course you are."

"I meant to see about the half-breeds."

"The three that are still alive will be here for some time, Dick."

"Which one is dead?"

"I don't know any of them."

"Did you notice one that was badly scarred from smallpox?"

"Yes. He's the dead man."

"He *is?*"

Roy nodded and asked, "Why?"

"That's Indian Pete! He's the chief troublemaker."

"Indian Pete," repeated Roy Rogers softly. He thought of the message with that name affixed, reposing in his wallet. "Who is Indian Pete?"

"I don't know much about him. He drifted in here a short time ago with the notion that he and some other half-breeds and Indians owned this land."

"Where did he get that idea?"

Dick shook his head. "I don't know," he said. "Maybe he read about some of those mixed-up land deals that've been in the paper. There were a couple of them in California."

Roy nodded, recalling one or two instances where a cloud had been cast on the title to land, due to early Spanish grants. "I know what you mean," he said, "but the Indians never *did* have title to land around here."

"That's just the point," agreed Dick. "Indian Pete must have been loco or something. He came here about a week and a half ago, told us the land was his and invited us to move out."

"Did he have any credentials to back his claim?"

Dick shook his head. "Not a thing. He got pretty ugly about it and Gimlet told him where to head in. He went away, and then we began getting notes."

"Notes? What kind of notes?"

"Warnings. He told us to get off the land or he'd put us off."

"Who *does* own the land?"

"A man in Gopher Creek, Lem Bixby, and his title is clear. We checked it before we bought the option. He has the deed to this land, and he'll turn it over to us with the search and survey whenever we take up the option."

"You figure on going right ahead with your work, eh?"

"Of course," replied Dick, as if the thought of quitting had never entered his head. "Why shouldn't we? The fire will set us back a little, but we'll bring in that oil or break our necks tryin'. If the derrick had gone up in smoke, we'd have been through, but I guess the fire didn't get that far."

"The derrick's unharmed," Roy informed him.

"I'll have to ride into Gopher Creek for more supplies," calculated Dick. "I'll borrow a little more cash from Abe Geesel." For the first time he realized that both he and Gimlet had kicked off their boots when they were settled in the house and had fought the battle in their stocking feet. With a wry smile at Roy he said, "Our boots were in the shack. I sure will look funny, ridin' into Gopher Creek without boots."

Roy remained quiet, wondering if he should tell

Dick about his brother now or wait until a little later.

Dick spoke again as his infectious sense of humor returned. "I shouldn't complain," he said. "I darn near died without my boots on."

A stirring came from the side of the lean-to where Gimlet lay. There was a muttering and mumbling, a grunt and a groan. Then Gimlet spoke and there was no weakness in his rasping voice.

"My carcass ain't nothin' but one big ache! I know the guys that's responsible. Where in blazes is my shootin' iron?"

CHAPTER SIX

Rogers laid a restraining hand on Gimlet's shoulder. "You'd better lie there on the blanket for a few minutes," he said. "You've been through a fight."

"Maybe I've been *in* a fight," snapped the old man, brushing Roy's hand aside, "but I ain't *through!* Not by a jugful! Just before they knocked me out, I was handlin' some business that ain't finished. I aim tuh finish it. I ain't through fightin' as long as I c'n stay perpendic'lar!" He struggled to a sitting position, groaned and held both hands against his head. He dropped back on the blanket and said in a less belligerent voice, "I—I ain't quite ready tuh git perpendic'lar. Gimme a couple o' minutes tuh git my bearin's an' I'll be up an' at 'em."

Roy smiled at Gimlet's courage.

"You can relax, Gimlet," said Dick. "Indian Pete is dead, and the others are tied up. We'll take them into Gopher Creek in the morning."

"Gopher Creek," growled Gimlet. "Why take 'em there?"

"We'll turn them over to the law."

"The law," spat Gimlet. "The law be hanged. *I'll* deal with them mangy, greasy-faced polecats. This is my fight an' I ain't fer lettin' the law horn in."

Dick grinned at Roy. "Isn't he a corker?" he asked. "He's as tough as a hickory nut."

Roy nodded and said, "He's terrific!"

"Gimme a drink," demanded Gimlet. He took a long pull at the canteen Roy uncapped and passed, returned the water container, wiped his mouth with his sleeve, and fixed his piercing eye on Roy.

"Who're you?" he asked.

Dick made the introduction. Gimlet looked at Roy, nodded briefly, and turned back to Dick.

"Did you say Pete was dead?" he asked.

"Yes."

Gimlet's face became distorted in a frightful way intended for a grin. "I hit him," he said simply. "That done it."

"No, that didn't do it, you conceited old bear-cat," Dick countered. "One of his men threw a knife at Roy, and Indian Pete got in the way."

Gimlet frowned. "Too bad," he growled. "I'd 'a' been proud to be the one that got that buzzard."

During this discussion Roy had taken the folded handkerchief from his wallet. He spread it out on the blanket, with the note opened for Dick to read. The time had come to break the news of Tom's death.

"Look at this, Dick. Does it look familiar?"

Dick propped himself up on an elbow to look at

the note and then at Roy. The grim expression on Roy's face, made grimmer by the ruddy glow of the embers that lighted the lean-to, must have told him something.

"Yes," he said. "That's the same sort of note we've been getting." He reached out a hand.

"Don't touch it, Dick," said Roy. "It may have fingerprints on it."

Dick swallowed hard. "Where did you get it?"

"I found it pinned to a man's shirt," said Roy softly. "The man was dead."

Dick looked at Roy. Their eyes met and held. Dick glanced at the note again. "Pinned to the shirt, eh?" A pause and then, "What kind of shirt?"

Roy took a fold of Dick's sleeve between his thumb and index finger. "Blue," he said. "Blue denim, just like this one."

Dick's swollen lips compressed. Gimlet had managed to sit up. He raked his stubby beard with one finger.

"He had hair like yours, Dick," Roy went on evenly. "In fact, he looked something like you."

Dick nodded slowly.

"I know," he whispered. "My brother—Tom." After a pause he asked, "How did they get him?"

"I don't think he knew what happened. It looked as if he'd been slugged from behind. There was nothing to show that he'd put up a fight."

"He would've fought if he'd had a chance."

Roy nodded. "I'm sure of that. That's why I say I don't think he knew what happened to him."

Roy didn't think it necessary, at least for the present, to give the rest of the details regarding Tom's death.

Now that the ice had been broken and Dick knew the worst, it was easy to go on. "I was coming from the west. I'd planned to camp in a little wood. That's where I found your brother. I didn't know who he was. Someone had gone through his pockets and cleaned them out. I didn't know how far I'd have to travel, so I couldn't bring him with me." Roy went on to explain how he had given Tom a burial as best he could. "We can have him moved to a permanent place, but I had to do something before I left him."

"There's no use sayin' thanks, Roy. I guess you know how I feel about what you did."

"Sure thing."

"You said something about fingerprints on the note."

"I suppose they'll match up with Indian Pete's, but it won't do any harm to have them checked to make sure."

Dick agreed.

Gimlet, much to the amazement of Roy and Dick, was on his feet. The tough old fellow's recovery was something at which to marvel. "I'll be back in a few minutes," Gimlet said.

"Where are you going?" demanded Dick.

"I gotta find my six-gun. I dropped it somewhere while I was fightin'."

"You won't need the gun tonight, Gimlet. Get back on the blanket. We'll find the gun in the morning, when it's light."

"The heck I won't need it tonight," retorted Gimlet. "How in thunder can I take care o' them three murderin' rats that're clutterin' up the ground an' foulin' up the air?"

"You're not going to get rid of them. I told you a few minutes ago that we'd take them into Gopher Creek in the morning."

"*You* told me, but I didn't agree tuh the scheme. Anyhow, that was *before*, an' this is *after*."

"What do you mean?"

"When I started out fer them a few minutes ago, it was on account of the way they came tuh git us an' the way they was tuh blame fer us losin' the shack. That was before I knowed about Tom. Wal, if I aimed tuh gun-kill 'em fer fightin' us, you c'n bet yer last doggoned thin dime I shore will finish 'em now that I know they're murderers!"

"No, Gimlet," pleaded Dick.

"I'll leave it tuh Rogers! He looks like a straight-thinkin' hombre. How about it, Rogers? Would you favor lettin' those critters go intuh the jail, an' then beat the case in trial because they's not enough evidence ag'in 'em? Of course, yuh wouldn't! You'd do the same as me. You'd finish the thing right here an' be sure of the way it come out."

"You're probably right, Gimlet," agreed Roy.

"There! Yuh see?" said the old man triumphantly.

"But there's just one thing," went on Roy.

"What's that?"

"Well, you see, it's going to be a mighty tough job to get this oil well finished. Now that's *one* thing that's got to be done. You owe it to Tom to bring the oil in."

"You bet I do! But what's that got tuh do with it?"

"It would be almost impossible for Dick to do the job alone."

"*Alone?* Without *me?* He couldn't do it! No, *sir!*"

Dick, realizing how Roy was working on Gimlet, kept quiet.

"You see," said Roy, "that's the angle you've got to consider. If you disposed of those half-breeds, taking the law into your own hands, you'd have to explain the whole thing to the sheriff in town. They might even hold you there for a few days, and Dick just couldn't get along if you weren't right here on the job."

Gimlet seemed to swell with importance.

"Doggone," he growled, "I never thought o' that angle. I suppose the sheriff *would* be fool enough tuh keep askin' me no end of questions an' things." He lowered his lean frame to the blanket, then stretched out. "I guess," he muttered, "Rogers is right. I ain't feelin' none too spry, anyhow."

CHAPTER SEVEN

PARTNERS

Knowing that Dick and Gimlet needed rest above all else, Roy suggested that they discuss their plans in the morning. His suggestion was accepted and his new-found friends stretched themselves out on the blanket beneath the tarpaulin.

Roy left the lean-to for a short tour of inspection before he, himself, turned in. He examined the captured men and made sure they suffered no undue hardship or pain from the lashings that insured against their escape. The four horses that had brought the attackers to the scene stood quietly near by. Roy led these into the corral where the two beasts belonging to Dick and Gimlet had been safe at a distance from the fire.

It took some time to unsaddle the half-breeds' horses. As Roy tossed each saddle over the top rail of the corral, he inspected the contents of the saddle-bags. He found nothing of interest in any of them except a supply of food which would come in handy at daybreak. His own supply wouldn't go far and he welcomed the addition.

After hanging the eatables from one of the braces of the derrick, where they'd be safe from small ani-

mals, he set out the utensils he'd need in the morning and then returned to the makeshift tent.

Neither Dick nor Gimlet stirred as Roy sat down
and pulled off his boots. Stretching out on the
blanket, he, too, was soon in the deep sleep of utter
exhaustion.

Gimlet's nostrils quivered at the tantalizing
aroma of fried bacon, coffee and hot biscuits. He
opened his eye and looked out on a gray, misty
morning. When he saw the source of the fragrant
odors he sat up abruptly and let out a howl of re-
sentment that jerked Dick from sound sleep to wide-
awake alertness.

"What's the matter with you?" demanded Dick.

Gimlet pointed out of the lean-to. "Look what's
goin' on!" he bellowed.

Dick saw the three half-breeds, their hands untied, squatting near a small fire. They were eating
griddle cakes, crisp bacon and fluffy biscuits and
washing the food down with coffee from tin cups.

Roy Rogers came into view with the freshly filled
canteen. "What's the howl about?" he grinned.

"Those critters!" roared Gimlet. "Those murderin',
half-breed polecats, eatin' our vittles!"

"What about it?" asked Dick. "They've got to
be fed!"

"They're eatin' better'n we've et fer the past three

weeks!"

"It's their own food," laughed Roy. "There's plenty for everyone. The batter's all mixed and ready for the flapjacks. Your chow will be ready in a jiffy."

Gimlet muttered beneath his breath. Though he had no more to say on the subject of the prisoners' breakfast, his dour expression showed that he considered it a wanton waste of good food. His mood improved after the first stack of buckwheat cakes. He passed his tin plate to Roy to be refilled. It was a compliment to Roy's cooking.

"Do you feel up to a ride to Gopher Creek?" asked the cowboy as he piled food on Gimlet's plate.

"Why shouldn't I? There's nothin' wrong with me."

Roy looked at the old man admiringly. "O.K.," he grinned.

"I suppose," said Gimlet, "you're still determined tuh take these critters in an' turn 'em over to the law?"

Roy nodded.

"I still think it'd be a sight simpler an' more complete tuh deal with 'em here."

"Don't be an old fool, Gimlet," put in Dick. "You can't do that sort of thing."

"Anyway," added Roy, "maybe they can tell a few things that'll help find the *real* troublemaker."

Dick looked up quickly. "The *real* troublemaker!" he repeated. "What do you mean, Roy?"

"I've been thinking over some of the things you told me," Roy explained.

"What things?"

"How you've been expecting to strike oil on this land so you could take up the option and buy it, and how Indian Pete kept still until just a few days ago."

"The chances are he didn't get the idea that he owned the land until a few days ago," said Dick.

"Let's look at it this way," Roy went on. "The man who owns this land never did anything with it. Then you come along and buy an option. You start drilling for oil and your prospects look mighty good. The owner realizes that he's got to sell you the land for a lot less than it's worth, and he doesn't want to do it!"

"So he tries tuh shag us," exploded Gimlet. "By Juniper, I wonder if *he* riled Injun Pete with the notion that he should run us out of here!"

"I hadn't thought of that," said Dick.

"Of course," explained Roy, "I'm just guessing, but it seems to me Indian Pete got stirred up mighty suddenly. I'd like to know who gave him the idea that he had a claim to this land."

Dick nodded slowly and said, "So would I."

"You're going to try to bring in the oil, aren't

"Indian Pete Got Stirred up Mighty Suddenly."

you?" asked Roy after a short pause.

"Sure thing. I'm going to call on Abe Geesel and talk him into laying out a little more cash. Then I'll get a couple of blankets and food enough to last us for a couple of weeks. I want to get a couple of repair parts for the engine and some tools, too. Then Gimlet and I will get to work as we've never worked before."

"Yer darn right," agreed Gimlet.

Roy stacked the plates and placed them in the skillet, ready for washing. "I've been wondering about something else," he said.

"What's that?"

"Aren't you going to be mighty shorthanded without your brother?"

"We sure are, but there isn't anything we can do about it, except work that much harder."

"Why not get another man to help you?"

Dick smiled wryly. "What'd we use for money to pay him?" he said.

"You could pay him after your well came in."

Dick shook his head slowly. "Men have a funny idea about workin' where there's only a slim chance of getting paid."

"Don't you expect to bring in the well?"

"We're going to try mighty hard," said Dick doggedly, "but there's no use kidding ourselves. The odds are against us."

"You might find a man who would take a chance with you."

"I don't know of any," he said.

"I do."

"You do? Who?"

"Me."

"*You!*" Dick stared at Roy. "Aw-w, you don't mean that, Roy."

"Why don't I mean it? What's the matter with me?" demanded the young cowboy. "Don't I look as if I could deliver a day's work?"

"Oh, sure you could! It isn't that. But we can't pay you anything, an' the work's hard, an' ..."

"Look here," broke in Roy, leaning nearer to Dick, "I was heading for some oil fields east of here to see how they're worked. I want to learn something about oil. Now it seems to me that I can learn more by watching you bring in a well than I can by watching one that's already in operation. I don't know how much help I'll be, but I'd like to hang around and do what I can."

"They's somethin' wrong somewhere," muttered Gimlet.

"What do you mean?"

The old man glared at Roy. "What're you after?" he demanded suspiciously. "You ain't needin' work so bad you gotta do it fer free."

"Experience," replied Roy.

"I dunno," said Gimlet.

"Button your lip, Gimlet," ordered Dick. To Roy he said, "I don't know why you're willing to pitch in with us, but I'm mighty glad to have you. We'll cut you in for the share Tom would've had."

"We can talk about that later on," replied Roy. "We've more important things to think of now. I'll get the horses saddled." He saw Dick's bootless feet. "Gosh!" he said. "I forgot that you and Gimlet had lost your boots in the fire. I've an extra pair that might fit you, but I don't know what we can do about Gimlet."

"Needn't worry about *me*," snorted the old man. "I'll cover *my* feet with boots." He stalked over to the three half-breeds near by and studied the boots of each one in turn. He squinted appraisingly, then advanced on the man in the center. "You," he said, "are ridin' tuh jail in yore stockin' feet!"

CHAPTER EIGHT

GOPHER CREEK

Gopher Creek, like many other western communities in the oil and cattle country, hadn't changed in fifty years. Electricity, telephones, even automobiles, had come without affecting the town's personality. A dirt road ran between two rows of one- and two-story buildings, and the usual saloons and dance halls waited all week for their night of tawdry gaiety on payday. There were a couple of stores, a church, a meeting hall and a small hotel. All of the buildings needed paint and wore a dry, parched look in the blistering sun of broad day.

Sheriff Lambert kept the peace of Gopher Creek, and kept it well. Swindlers and confidence men had long since learned to keep away from his town. The sheriff had an eagle eye that spotted most crooks before they could settle themselves. It was because of the efficiency of Jim Lambert that crime in Gopher Creek was so much less than that of other communities of equal size.

There was another thing about the law in Gopher Creek. It worked quickly and efficiently. When a man landed in jail, he stayed there until his trial, which was never long delayed. There were few instances in which men were released on bail. Lambert had ways of discouraging the practice.

Lem Bixby lived in Gopher Creek. Dick Collins pointed out his small house near the edge of town.

"You two shove on and turn the half-breeds over to the law," suggested Roy. "I'll stop off here and get acquainted with Bixby."

"O.K.," agreed Dick.

As Roy reined up beside the porch and swung to the ground, the front door opened and two men appeared. Lem Bixby, small and stout, was in his shirtsleeves. The other man wore a suit which had, when new, been black, but age had turned it to a greenish hue. His face was lean and hawklike, with eyes set far back beneath shaggy brows.

"Come again," called Bixby as the lean man in black went down the steps from the porch. Then he saw Roy Rogers. "You lookin' fer someone?" he called.

Roy said, "I'm looking for Lem Bixby. I guess you're the man, aren't you?"

"Right."

Roy stepped onto the porch. "They tell me," he said, "that you've some land a few miles from here."

"What about it?"

"Is it for sale?"

"Might be, then again, it might not be."

Roy nodded and said, "Let's talk it over."

Bixby said, "Come on in."

Roy entered the neat house. He had seized on the handiest reason to spend a few minutes with Bixby. He wasn't interested in land. He *was* interested in Bixby. He wanted a chance to size Bixby up and decide whether he might be capable of inciting Indian Pete and the other half-breeds to murder.

The jail was solidly built. A long, wide hall ran its entire length. In this hall there were benches, a table, and a couple of chairs for the use of the guards. On each side of the hall there was a row of small cells, each with one window and a door, both heavily barred.

Gimlet and Dick accompanied the sheriff when he locked the three half-breeds in one cell, then went with him to the coroner's office next door to dispose of the body of Indian Pete.

They continued on to the next building where Sheriff Lambert had his office. Here they made their statements and swore to them before a deputy who witnessed their signatures.

Gimlet looked at a smudge of ink on his thumb. He licked it, then wiped it on the seat of his trousers.

"I guess that settles the killers, don't it, Sheriff?" he asked.

"It does as far as you're concerned," replied Lambert. "It all depends on the outcome of their trial.

I've got to make an investigation. Have to bring Tom's body in and attend to a lot of details, then we'll put the prisoners on trial. If they're found guilty, the chances are they'll hang."

"Hold on," snapped Gimlet. "What d'you mean, *if* they're found guilty? We know they're guilty. There ain't no doubt about it, is there?"

Sheriff Lambert smiled at the old man. "Take it easy, Gimlet," he said. "You've done your part."

"I handed yuh the note that was pinned tuh Tom's shirt," went on Gimlet. "If that ain't enough proof, look at the way me an' Dick are battered up, an' then ride out an' look at the pile of ashes where our shack stood."

Dick interrupted the violent old man. "The sheriff will see that justice is done," he said.

"I was afraid they'd be somethin' tuh keep them critters from hangin'," Gimlet grumbled. "Hang it all, I should o' shot 'em last night when I had the chance. All this delay is just a waste o' time. I wish I'd shot the polecats."

"If you had," replied the sheriff evenly, "I'd have had to throw you into jail, Gimlet."

"Me?" howled the old man.

"Yes, you. Now get out of here before I decide to jug you as a material witness."

Gimlet's face was a study in bewilderment.

"What uz that?" he demanded. "D'you mean tuh

say that you could toss me intuh the calaboose because I'm a *witness?*"

The sheriff, who knew and understood the old man, suppressed a desire to grin, and nodded seriously. "You bet I could," he said.

Gimlet spat on the floor and turned to Dick. "C'mon," he said. "Let's git out o' here before this galoot starts tryin' tuh hang *me*. I never seen the like of it."

The two strode from the office with Gimlet still complaining. "What we need around here is some Vigilantes or somethin'," he grumbled. "This place is gettin' too dang much law."

"The sheriff was right," explained Dick, as he closed the door behind him. "There's no use getting steamed up. The breeds will get what's coming to them."

But Gimlet refused to be mollified. "Time was," he said, "when an honest man's word was taken by honest lawmen. Blast it all, Dick, we've been insulted, that's what!"

"Insulted?"

"Sure! If Lambert had believed us, he'd o' let it go at that, but he didn't believe us. He's got tuh prove things fer himself. Why, dang it all, that's the same as sayin' that me an' you didn't tell the truth." Gimlet was working himself up to a fine fury. He stopped in his tracks as a new realization struck him.

"See here! It just dawned on me!" he roared. "Sheriff Lambert as much as called me a downright liar. I won't take that from no man!" He turned and started back.

Dick grabbed Gimlet's arm and said, "*Now* where are you goin'?"

"I gotta call that lawman! I won't stand fer bein' called a liar!"

"Gimlet," said Dick, "I've got to call on Abe Geesel. Why don't you go to the Silver Dollar and see if any of your old pals are around?"

Gimlet's eye lighted at the suggestion. "I'll go tell 'em how Lambert insulted me," he said.

"Sure! That's the idea. See what they have to say about it."

Gimlet nodded, and headed for the café a few doors down the street.

Dick watched his old friend shuffle away, then turned, and with a grim expression on his face started toward Abe Geesel's office.

CHAPTER NINE

AN UNEXPECTED BLOW

News travels fast in a town the size of Gopher Creek. Soon after Dick and Gimlet rode into the community, their arrival was general knowledge. Nearly everyone in town soon knew the details of Tom's murder and Indian Pete's death, as well as the story of the fire at the derrick and the capture of the half-breeds.

Abe Geesel heard the items of news from the hard lips of a man who came to his office on the second floor of the building across from the sheriff's office. It was a musty, dingy room overlooking the street. A film of dust on the window made it almost impossible for sunlight to enter the room. There was a battered old desk which had known many owners before Abe Geesel parted with two dollars to acquire it. The chair with it didn't swivel any more. It was slightly lopsided for lack of a caster and would tip over if an unsuspecting occupant leaned too far back. Geesel had bought the chair with the desk for two bits extra. A battered old file cabinet and an iron safe were the only other pieces of office equipment. They were grouped at one side of the window. Geesel lived on the other side. His dirty-

blanketed cot stood against the wall beside a table.
A shelf over the table held the few supplies Geesel
needed for his simple fare. The room was odorous
with a combination of mustiness and sweat, rank
coffee and the characteristic smell of a coal-oil
burner. The floor and walls were bare and dirty.

The man who stood at Geesel's side at the window was known as Snag Pritchard. He, like Geesel,
would do anything for a price. The only difference
lay in his way of doing it. Geesel, cowardly as he
was shrewd, hired others to do his rough work.
Pritchard, bold and not very shrewd, was the type
of man he hired.

"I hope you've got the facts straight, Pritchard,"
said Abe Geesel.

"It's just like I told yuh," the hard-faced man
replied. "The shack is burned an' Tom is dead.
Indian Pete can't talk because he's dead, too."

A smug look of satisfaction crossed Abe Geesel's
face as he watched Dick Collins and Gimlet leave
the sheriff's office. He knew nothing about the help
Roy Rogers had given the pair. He had seen the
young cowboy at Lem Bixby's house, but there was
no reason to associate him with the two across the
street.

"All right," he told Pritchard. "If you're sure of
the facts, you know what you're to do. You'd better
get out of here before Collins comes up."

"Don't forget what you offered me," warned Pritchard.

"You'll get your hundred dollars when you've done the job."

"I'll be back here to collect before sundown," replied the one called Snag. "You'd better have it ready for me."

"It'll be ready. Now get out. Collins is coming across the street."

Pritchard nodded and glanced out the window. The sight of Gimlet heading for the Silver Dollar gave him an idea. He grinned and stroked his chin.

"See yuh soon," he muttered, and left the room.

As Pritchard closed the door of Geesel's office, he heard Dick's footsteps starting up the stairs. To avoid a meeting he hurried down a narrow corridor running the entire length of the building. There was a window at the end of the corridor where the shade had been drawn to keep out the sun. Snag hugged the wall, waiting in the darkness.

Dick rapped on the thin door.

"Come in," said Geesel.

The moneylender sat at his desk when Dick entered the room. He nodded formally and pointed to a battered chair.

"Sit down," he said. "Has the well come in?"

Dick shook his head and said, "Not yet."

"Not yet?"

"Nope. The prospects look better all the time though, and I'm pretty sure we'll get the oil in a few days."

"Your time is short."

"I know that, Mr. Geesel. We've sunk the shaft over a thousand feet now. We're just about ready to try a blast and see if that won't start the oil."

"It seems to me you're wasting valuable time," said Geesel. "The time it took for you to ride to town and the time it will take to return to the job might have been better spent in work."

Dick felt anger rise within him at the surly manner of the moneylender.

"We came to town to turn in the men who murdered my brother," he said shortly.

"Tom?"

"Yes."

"How did it happen?"

"Indian Pete got the idea that he owned the land. He made a few threats but we didn't take them seriously. Then he and three of his friends met Tom on the trail and killed him!"

"Where did this happen?" asked Geesel.

Dick told him.

"What was he doing so far from the job?"

"He took a couple of days to call on some friends."

"Humph. If he'd been on the job where he belonged, it wouldn't have happened."

Dick's cheeks burned with anger which was becoming increasingly hard to suppress. His fists were clenched with the effort to restrain himself. There was an edge, hard and cold as steel, in his voice.

"After the murderers finished Tom, they came for Gimlet and me," he said. "There was a fight in the shack and the lamp was knocked over. The shack burned to the ground."

"How about the derrick?" inquired Geesel, although he already knew the details from Pritchard.

"The derrick is all right."

"Then there's nothing to keep you from going back to work, is there?"

"I told you," said Dick as evenly as possible, "that we'd lost the shack and everything in it. That means clothes and blankets, even our grub."

"I see," replied Geesel.

"We need a little more cash to see us through."

"So that's why you came to me?"

"Yes. And while we're at it, we'd better get a couple of drills. We've broken all but one, going through hard rock. We should have at least one spare."

Geesel tapped the tips of his fingers together and frowned. "I told you when you started," he said, "to figure out just how much cash you'd need for your enterprise. It was upon the amount you needed that I based my decision to back you. I didn't expect you to come back, demanding additional money."

Dick hated himself for not smashing the loathsome creature between the eyes. He was hot and humiliated and the rank odors of the room disgusted him.

"I didn't foresee what was going to happen," he said.

"You should have!" Geesel assumed a patronizing manner. "Young man, to get ahead in this world you've got to foresee every contingency. Alibis won't put money in the bank!"

"Look here, Mr. Geesel," said Dick. "I need about a hundred dollars to see me through. I might squeeze by with less. I'd sooner do *anything* than come to you asking for more money, but I had to do it. Gimlet and I are willing to sleep without a shelter and take our chances on the weather. We're willing to work as many hours as we can and get by with just enough food to keep us going. But we've *got* to get a few parts for the engine and we've got to get a spare drill." He leaned back in the creaking chair. "That's all there is to it," he finished.

"You speak of money as if it grew on trees. A hundred dollars, indeed!"

Geesel opened the warped drawer of the desk. It stuck and he had to jerk it. He drew out a bluebound paper. "I," he said, "have been looking through this contract between us."

"There's a Mistake Somewhere," Dick Said Heatedly

Dick recognized the legal form, and nodded.

"My copy is in the sheriff's office," he said. "It's a lucky thing it wasn't in the shack, or I'd have lost that, too."

Geesel went on as if Dick hadn't spoken. He flicked the paper with his fingers. "As I said, I've been going over this contract, Collins. I'm not satisfied with the deal!"

"Not satisfied!" exclaimed Dick. "I don't see where you've got any complaint. You lent us a little cash and we're to pay you back with interest. On top of that you get a quarter interest in the oil well!"

"If," said Geesel, "you strike oil. I don't think you will. I have reports that indicate we all made a mistake in our choice of a place to drill. I've put all the cash I intend to lose into the proposition. I see no reason to throw good money after bad."

Dick was on his feet. This was something upon which he hadn't counted. Had he gone through the torture of this humiliating interview, only to be turned down?

"There's a big mistake somewhere," he said heatedly. "I don't know where you got your reports, but I say they're all wrong. The prospects for oil look better than at any time."

Geesel shook his head slowly.

"Do you mean to say," demanded Dick, "that you

won't risk another fifty dollars or so to save all you've put into the thing so far?"

"I don't *mean* to say it," Geesel retorted. "I *have* said it."

He turned to his desk and pretended to be absorbed in other matters.

CHAPTER TEN

GUNFIRE

Roy Rogers and Lem Bixby were drawn together almost as soon as they shook hands. Bixby was an easy-going man with a straightforward manner. His eyes were blue and honest and his face was crinkled from many years of easy laughter.

When Roy inquired about the land on which Dick Collins held an option, Bixby gave him the details without reservation. He had, he explained, suspected that the ground held oil, but had never felt inclined to investigate. His income was sufficient for his needs and simple luxuries and he chose to enjoy what he had rather than to assume the worry and responsibility accompanying acquisition of more money. He had welcomed the chance to sell his land at a fair price, and hoped Dick would strike oil and make huge profits on the investment.

"I'm sorry the lad went to Abe Geesel for money," he said. "Not that I know anything against Geesel. It's just that Dick and Tom and their old pal would be better off if they hadn't cut someone else in on the deal."

Then Roy told about Tom's death and the subsequent battle at the derrick. Bixby was shocked immeasurably by the news.

"I came to see you," Roy said frankly, "because I had a hunch you might've been mixed up in the murder."

Bixby's eyes went wide in amazement.

"You see, Bixby," Roy went on, "Collins has done a lot of work. He has a first-rate derrick, and the shaft is down about a thousand feet. If he doesn't take up the option, you can put some men to work and bring the well in for yourself."

"And—and you think I fed Indian Pete a lot of lies to start him on a murder trail?"

"I don't think so," Roy smiled. "In fact, I'm sure you didn't. I said I came here because I *had* a hunch. That was before I knew you."

"I'm glad you've changed your mind!"

Roy nodded and said, "I have."

"Your reasoning was logical enough, Roy. But there's one good reason why I wouldn't pull a scurvy trick like that."

"You couldn't," said Roy. "You're not the type."

"There's another reason. I wouldn't benefit as you thought."

"You wouldn't?"

Bixby shook his head. "There's a second option on the land. If Dick doesn't buy it, a man named Clayton has a chance at it."

"Who's he?"

"I don't know. I never met him. He's no one
around here. He did his business through Luther
Abercrombie, the lawyer here in Gopher Creek."

"I wonder," said Roy slowly, "if Clayton gave
Indian Pete a few ideas?"

"It might be a good idea to investigate that
angle," suggested Bixby. "I'll help in any way I
can."

Roy said, "I'll look around."

"Do you think the three half-breeds might be
made to talk? Maybe they could tell who gave
Pete the idea that he owned land."

"I tried to talk to them last night," replied Roy.
"They didn't seem to know anything at all. Maybe
the sheriff can loosen their tongues."

"Roy," said Lem Bixby, "what's Dick going to
do? Is he going to quit?"

"Not if he can help it. He and Gimlet are going
on with their work. I'm going to give them what
help I can. I don't think I can do much, but I'm
going to try."

"I'm glad to hear that. I'll do anything I can for
them."

When, some time later, Roy rose to leave, he and
Bixby were warm friends. They shook hands, and a
moment later Roy was in the saddle heading for
the heart of town.

He had remained with Bixby much longer than

he had intended. He measured the time of day against Dick's schedule and calculated that he'd find Collins at Abe Geesel's office. He reined up in front of the general store and dismounted. Tossing the reins over Trigger's head, he lopped them about the hitchrail.

Roy was just about to start up the stairs to Geesel's office when his attention was caught by a burst of laughter from across the street. He turned quickly and saw the source. The door of the Silver Dollar stood wide open. Gimlet was just inside, surrounded by a group of friends and apparently having the time of his life.

Roy smiled and started up the stairs.

With his hand on the knob of the door that led to Geesel's office, he paused. Dick's voice, fairly trembling with emotion, came through the thin door sharply.

"Look here!" cried Dick. "Without cash we can't go on! You can't pull a deal like this, Geesel!"

"Who can't?" snapped a reedy, unpleasant voice. "Don't you tell *me* what I can or cannot do. I know my rights and I know the law! I also know what's in our contract! If you can't continue without additional funds, Collins, you'll simply have to quit! That's all there is to it! Now get out of here and leave me alone. I'm busy."

"*Quit!*" Dick roared. "We can't quit now. We're

on the home stretch. We've only a couple of weeks more before the option runs out, and we're right on the verge of getting oil. We *can't* quit now. There's oil in that ground and we're going to get it!"

"Well, then," sneered Geesel, "go right ahead and get it, but you'll have to do it without *my* money."

"I'll get money! I'll find someone to lend me what I need."

"Oh, no, you won't! If you'll read over the contract, you'll see that I have the exclusive right to finance you."

Roy Rogers opened the door. Abe Geesel sat in his chair, turned sideways to the desk, looking at Dick Collins with a smug expression. Dick stood, his fists clenched at his sides and his face white with anger. Neither of the two saw the young cowboy.

Geesel held a contract in his hand. He pointed to this as he spoke. "If you've forgotten what the contract says, I'll let you borrow my copy and you can read it over. You can't borrow a cent of cash from anyone else, Collins. Neither can you accept help in the form of material or supplies in lieu of cash! I have the exclusive right to finance your undertaking and, if you get help elsewhere, I'll tie you up with injunctions and restraining orders so you'll not be able to lift a hand."

Dick's throat muscles throbbed with emotion. His voice was tremulous with an anger that seethed inside and threatened to explode into violent action at any instant.

"You mean to say that you not only won't let us have the things we need, you'll keep us from getting them anywhere else?"

"Young man," said Geesel in that paternal manner he used occasionally, "I've tried to explain that you should have taken every angle into consideration when you made your estimate of costs. You told me you needed a certain amount of money and I gave it to you. If you'd said, at the time, that you needed more, I might not have gone into the proposition in the first place."

"You didn't give me what I asked for in the first place," Dick retorted hotly. "You cut it down, and you know it!"

"You said you thought you could get by with what you had."

"I could have, if it hadn't been for the murder and the fire!"

"Alibis won't go in business," said Geesel, shaking his head. "I was afraid you were too optimistic about what you could do. I've often seen young, enthusiastic chaps like you blind themselves to reality by their enthusiasm. You made a mistake, Collins. You undertook too big a job."

"It wasn't—" began Dick.

Geesel silenced the outburst with a wave of his hand. "You made a mistake in your calculations, Collins. You can't deny it. If you hadn't made a mistake, you wouldn't be here now. You'd be working at your well. Your mistake has cost me considerable money. I don't hold that against you. You'll not have to repay what you borrowed. Now you want permission to borrow cash elsewhere, and you are angry at me because I won't give you that permission."

Geesel cleared his throat before he went on. "There are legal angles that you, perhaps, don't understand. The only way you can borrow money is by putting up security. You have no security. You would have to borrow money on the future prospects of the oil well, and this would be a legal encumbrance on the property." Geesel then tossed in a few legal phrases and complicated sentences that meant nothing to either Dick or Roy Rogers, still standing unnoticed at the door. "There is no use discussing the matter any further," Geesel finished. "You will profit by this experience. I have no doubt made you despise me, but the day will come when you will thank me."

The smug hypocrisy of the moneylender infuriated Roy as much as it did Dick Collins.

"I see through your whole scheme," Dick said

bitterly. "It's as plain as day."

"My scheme?"

"You know what I mean! You wouldn't lend us as much as I said we'd need. You beat me down to the point where you were sure I couldn't bring in the oil. I took your proposition because there was nothing else I could do. Then the three of us worked like blazes, just as you knew we'd work! We bought a lot of broken-down equipment and made the best of it. We worked sixteen to twenty hours a day, and half the time we were repairing the old engine or splicing cables. Right from the start you didn't intend to let us bring in the oil. You figured on waiting for us to do most of the work, then freezing us out."

"Tut, tut, young man. I can understand how bitter you feel, but I cannot let you make any more unfair accusations."

"Well, that's one thing you can't stop me from doing!" retorted Dick hotly. "You saw that we were likely to get the oil in spite of the small amount of cash we had to work with! You began to worry about it! It wouldn't surprise me one bit to learn that you're back of the murder of my brother."

"That's preposterous," barked Geesel. His suave manner fell away like a cloak. He smashed his fist down on the desk and his parchment-like face distorted with rage. "Don't you call me a murderer!"

"Someone got Indian Pete stirred up," replied Dick. "I'm going to find out who it was!"

"You—"

"And there's another thing I'm going to find out," declared Dick. "I'm going to see if there's a second option on that land! I'm going to find out if you aren't planning to grab it just as soon as I lose my chance to get it!"

"You're a fool!" howled Geesel.

"And you," snapped Dick, "are a scheming rat! I don't know why I didn't suspect it before this! It's as clear as crystal! If I can get those half-breeds to talk, I'll bet my neck they'll say that you're the one who incited Indian Pete! If that's the case, Geesel, you'll *hang!*"

"You can't call me names and get away with it, Collins! I'll have the law on you!"

"If you *are* the one who's back of my brother's murder, you'd better start crawling for a hole!"

"I've taken enough from you," shrilled Geesel. His hand came up from beneath the desk gripping a heavy gun. "I'll not let you or anyone else call me a murderer!"

Dick Collins didn't realize how he had infuriated Abe Geesel. He didn't know that the statements he'd made had hit so close to the bull's-eye that Geesel had gone blind in the panic of abject fear. He saw the gun, and thought of it as nothing but a threat. He didn't know there was murder in Abe Geesel's mind.

It was Roy who saw that Geesel meant to fire. He correctly interpreted the cold film that came over Geesel's eyes, and saw the muscles in the trigger finger tighten. It all happened in an instant. Roy acted instinctively. His hand dropped to his holster, too fast for the eye to follow. He fired while the barrel of his gun was clearing the holster. Close on the heels of the pistol shot, there was a smack of lead on steel. Geesel's weapon leaped from his hand like a living thing, spun in the air, and fell across the room.

Geesel screamed in wild surprise and fear, then stood staring, wild-eyed and speechless.

"Roy!" gasped Dick Collins in surprise.

Before anything else could be said, the sound of shooting came from across the street. There were several shots, with shrill cries of terror sandwiched between them. The next instant brought a confusion of yells and cries. Roy glanced through the dirty window and saw men running from all directions, converging on the jail.

"Come on!" he cried to Dick. He dropped his gun into the holster, wheeled quickly, and dashed for the stairs.

CHAPTER ELEVEN

TRIPLE KILLING

A crowd of milling, excited men gathered at the jail, tightly packed in the ten-foot alley running along one side of the prison. They stood on tiptoe, stretching their necks in an effort to look into the small, barred window of one of the cells. They were jammed close together, fifteen or twenty deep, at the front of the jail, trying to see through the open door. There was a hubbub of clacking voices. Each new arrival shouted question after question. Those who had arrived a moment earlier were proud to supply answers to the questions in equally loud voices.

Sheriff Lambert came from his office, two doors away on a dead run. He hit the fringe of the crowd, then fought his way, shouldering and elbowing, toward the door. A deputy holding a gun in each hand stepped aside to let the lawman enter, then quickly resumed his post to hold back the morbidly curious mob.

Roy Rogers and Dick Collins learned the cause of the excitement soon after their arrival. They didn't need to ask questions. They had only to listen.

96

The three half-breeds, who had been locked in a single cell, had been wantonly murdered in cold blood.

The town had been in the calm of early afternoon on a hot day. The horses at the hitchrails stood languidly, brushing their tails against droning insects. Dogs slept in the shade of the buildings. A few men, their feet on the railing, sat quietly smoking on the hotel veranda.

The guard, seated at a table in the central section of the jail, had been listening to the drone of conversation from the Silver Dollar, a few doors down the street. He had heard something that sounded like a gunshot, but it was distant and muffled. He had risen from his chair and sauntered to the open door, where he glanced both ways on the street without seeing cause for agitation. Soon after resuming his place at the table, he heard the sharp crack of a gunshot close at hand.

These had snapped the man to his feet. There were shrill cries from the cell where the half-breeds were confined, then several more shots. By the time Mart Merkle reached the cell, the men inside were sprawled in grotesque positions on the floor. It had taken a moment to unlock the door and another moment to confirm the fact that the prisoners were dead.

The mob had formed as if by magic.

Roy and Dick looked at each other. The murder of the half-breeds was significant.

"I guess," muttered Dick, "those critters knew more than we suspected."

Roy nodded grimly, wishing he had been more insistent when he had questioned them the night before.

"I wonder," he said softly, "where Gimlet is?"

Dick shook his head slowly and replied, "I hope he's with friends in the Silver Dollar."

As if to answer Roy's question, there was a sudden increase of excitement in the alley. Two stern-faced deputies came from the rear of the building, holding Gimlet between them. The old man was a squirming, struggling bundle of violent action. He snorted and howled protestations of innocence. He maligned the law and those who represented it. He tried to hold back, he braced his feet, and, when the lawmen lifted him off the ground, his wiry legs worked like pistons gone wild. He kicked and fought each step of the way.

The sympathies of the crowd were with the old man. There were shouts of encouragement to Gimlet and demands that the lawmen let him go and pick someone their own size.

Ultimately his captors reached the door and dragged Gimlet into the jail.

"We'd better get in there," Roy suggested. "The

‚old man is in trouble."

Dick nodded silently.

The men ahead, knowing Dick's relationship to Gimlet, quickly made way.

When Dick and the cowboy reached the door, the guard admitted them, then slammed the door and said, "No more in here!"

Sheriff Lambert sat at the table, Gimlet in front of him, glaring balefully at his captors.

"We'll see that he doesn't make any more trouble," said Dick.

"You handle the old critter," said one of the deputies, stepping back. "You're welcome to him. I've handled men three times his weight with less trouble!"

Dick stepped to his old friend's side. Roy took up a position on the other side and laid a reassuring hand on Gimlet's shoulder.

"Take it easy," he said softly.

"They're tryin' tuh say that I shot them breeds," howled Gimlet indignantly. "If I'd o' done it, I wouldn't lie about it. I'd brag about it! But dagnab it all, I didn't shoot 'em! I admit I wanted tuh, but I didn't!"

"Quiet down," commanded the sheriff. "Someone killed the three prisoners by pourin' lead through the window. I'm goin' to find the man that did it and he's goin' to pay!"

"Why are yuh yappin' at me?" barked Gimlet.

"Gimlet!" said the lawman. "Where's your gun?"

"Where in tunket d'ya think it is? It's right where I allus keep it in case I—" He broke off abruptly and his mouth hung open. He looked down at the holster, hanging empty, on his belt. "It—it's gone," he finished hollowly. "My shootin' iron is gone."

The sheriff pointed to the pistol on the table before him. "Is that it?" he asked.

Gimlet glanced at the weapon. He reached for it, but the sheriff drew it back.

"I was just goin' to look at 'er," Gimlet explained. "It's my gun, if it's got my name cut on the handle. If it ain't got my name, it ain't."

"Your name is on it," the sheriff replied grimly.

"Where'd you get it?"

"Inside the cell where the half-breeds were killed."

"*What?*" howled Gimlet. "I been framed!"

The sheriff opened the gun and showed the cap ends of the cartridges.

"All six of them have been fired," he said. Turning to Matt Merkle, he asked, "How many shots did you say there were?"

"I wasn't sure about the first one, Sheriff. It could have been a long way off, or near by. It was muffled. It seemed to come from somewhere across the street, though."

Roy knew the guard referred to the shot he'd fired in disarming Abe Geesel.

"The rest of the shots were right near by," the guard went on. "There were five or six of them. I can't be dead sure."

"But there might have been six?"

Matt nodded.

"Six shots," said the sheriff, turning back to Gimlet, "have been fired from this gun."

"I never was inside that pertickler cell in my life!" roared Gimlet.

"The shots came through the window."

"Listen tuh me!" barked Gimlet. "D'you think I'd be fool enough tuh toss my gun inside the cell after I'd drilled those buzzards? Guns don't grow on trees! Neither does the cash tuh buy 'em. I had that shootin' iron fer a good many years an' I think a lot of it. I wouldn't throw it away! I ain't loco."

"You might have dropped it after the last shot," said the sheriff. "And, of course, if you did, you couldn't reach it."

"*Me?*" snapped Gimlet. "*Me* drop a gun? Humph! That's an insult."

"We can send the gun and the death slugs to the city and have 'em checked, Gimlet. We can prove whether or not they came from your gun."

"I ain't denyin' that fact. They probably did! But I didn't fire 'em."

"Who did?"

"How in blazes do I know?"

"Where were you when the shots were fired?" asked the sheriff.

Gimlet shook his head and said, "I dunno."

This curious statement brought murmurs of surprise from the men in the room. Dick nudged his old friend and whispered in his ear, "Don't be an old fool, Gimlet. Tell the sheriff the truth."

Gimlet glowered at Dick. "I am tellin' the truth," he said indignantly. "What's more I'm gettin' dang tired of standin' here. My feet hurt like sin." As an afterthought he muttered, "I wish that breed had wore bigger boots."

Sheriff Lambert slapped the table with his open hand. "Do you," he roared, "mean to say you don't know where you were when those shots were fired?"

"That's what I said," retorted Gimlet. "I dunno where I was because I didn't hear the shots. Now stop yellin' at me. I ain't deaf."

"You didn't *hear* them?"

"No!"

Jim Lambert came to his feet with such speed that his chair spilled backward, slamming against the floor. "Y-You," he cried, shaking his finger toward Gimlet, "listen to me!"

"Huh?"

"Those shots were heard from Lem Bixby's house

"Where Were You When the Shots Were Fired?"

at one end of town to Widow Parker's at the other!
Job Fisher heard 'em inside his blacksmith shop an'
Dick Halpern heard 'em in the hotel. Everyone in
town heard that gunplay! D'you expect me to believe you didn't hear them?"

The sheriff's face was purple when he finished his
outburst.

"*Answer me!*"

"You bet I will!" retorted Gimlet. He brought his
calloused hand down flat on the top of the table in
a "splat" that sounded like a pistol's crack. "I c'n
yowl as loud as you or the next man," he began. "I
don't expect you tuh believe nothin'. What's more
I don't give three hoots of an owl if you believe what
I say or not! It don't matter a doggone bit tuh me
what you believe! If you warn't such a cussed, stubborn, all-knowin' smart aleck—"

At this point Gimlet shook himself free of Dick
and Roy. He growled, "Lemme alone. I gotta tell
this upstart lawman." Then he continued where he
had left his speech suspended. "—If you warn't such
a dimwit, you'd stop pesterin' me an' go catch a few
murderers! You asked where I was when the shots
was fired an' I told yuh I didn't know! That was the
truth. How do I know where I was when I didn't hear
the shots? Maybe *you* can hear things while you're
sleepin'. That wouldn't surprise me a bit, on account
of the size of yer ears. But I can't!"

"Hold on," the sheriff broke in when Gimlet paused for a breath. "Do you mean to say you were sleeping?"

"Yes!"

The sheriff sat down limply in the chair someone had righted. "Why," he gasped, "why in heaven's name didn't you say you were sleepin'?"

"You didn't ask me," retorted the old man.

"But, wait, you at least know where you were sleeping!"

"When the shots was fired?"

The sheriff nodded. "Yes," he said. "Where were you sleeping?"

Gimlet shook his head slowly. "Son," he said, "y'got me."

"What d'you mean by that?"

"I dunno."

The lawman put the flat of both hands against his temples, holding his head tightly while he closed his eyes.

"I slept in at least two places," went on Gimlet, by way of explanation. "There may've been more. D'you want me to explain how it come about?"

The speechless sheriff managed to nod.

"I was in the Silver Dollar," Gimlet began. I was just standin' thar, chewin' the rag with my friends. Someone slid a drink before me. I gulped 'er fast, an' went on talkin'. Then I got gosh-awful tired so

I moseyed tuh the back room where I sat down in a chair tuh rest fer a little while. Next thing I knew, a couple of yore deputies," Gimlet paused at this point to glare balefully at his captors, "a couple of yore deputies," he went on, "had me by the arms, draggin' me through a crowd an' yappin' somethin' about the shootin' o' the half-breeds. I went tuh sleep in the Silver Dollar an' woke up in the hands o' them galoots."

The sheriff looked at the deputies. "Where did you find him?" he asked.

"He was in the shade back of the jail, stretched on the ground up close to the building."

"Y'see!" said Gimlet. "Thar's at least two places where I slept an' there may've been more. Now how in blazes do I know where I was when them murder shots was fired?" He gazed around the room with a triumphant gleam in his red-rimmed eye.

The sheriff turned to his deputy and said, "Was he sleeping when you found him?"

"Sound asleep and snoring his head off."

Jim Lambert nodded.

Roy Rogers wanted to speak, but thought he'd wait to see how things developed. He was delighted when the sheriff began summarizing the situation.

"It seems to me," began the lawman, "that the facts are pretty clear. Someone wanted to rub out the half-breeds. Whoever it was knew that Gimlet had had a-plenty to say about shootin' them, and figured it would be a simple matter to frame the old man."

There were mutters of agreement.

The sheriff continued. "Someone, the murderer no doubt, saw to it that Gimlet got a doped drink in the Silver Dollar. It would be easy to drop a little powder in any drink that stood handy and slide it before Gimlet. He waited in the back of the café until Gimlet passed out, then dragged him here to the jail to make it tough for Gimlet to prove an alibi. He borrowed the old man's gun and shot the half-breeds. Then he left the gun and scooted, leaving Gimlet to face the music."

"That's it," applauded Gimlet. "That's just it, sheriff! You got more brains than I gave yuh credit for!"

The sheriff had summarized the plot to everyone's satisfaction. Roy Rogers was glad the lawman saw through the frameup and believed in Gimlet's innocence.

"What about me?" demanded Gimlet. "Am I tuh be let go, or jugged?"

"You c'n go," the sheriff said. "We won't hold you."

"What about my gun?" asked Gimlet, pointing to the weapon on the table.

"It's being held as evidence."

"Evidence fer what? You know the breeds are

dead, an' you know they got shot by my gun. What else is there tuh prove by holdin' the hardware?"

"It's evidence to be used at the trial of the murderer," the sheriff said, with admirable restraint. "You'll get your gun back when we're through with it."

"You mean after the trial?"

"Yes."

"But the trial can't start until yuh find the murderer!"

Lambert shook his head patiently.

Gimlet gathered himself for another explosive outburst, but Jim Lambert cooled him when he said, "Gimlet, I'm letting you go, but if I want to, I can hold you in jail as a suspect. I might even put you on trial for the murder—if I wanted to. Now you'd better clear out of here before I change my mind. Don't let me hear any more arguments."

"Come on, Gimlet," said Dick, taking his friend's arm.

Roy, on Gimlet's other side, left the jail with his friends.

Roy Rogers was glad to get away from the inquisition. There were investigations he wanted to make on his own hook. He recalled Abe Geesel's frenzy when Dick had charged him with the murder of the first half-breed, Indian Pete. The moneylender had acted like a guilty man. Of course, Geesel had an alibi for the shooting of the three prisoners, but he might easily have deputized someone for this job, just as Indian Pete had been deputized to kill Tom.

There was another name that clung to Roy's mind. The name was Clayton, the unknown individual who had, through Abercrombie, bought the second option on Lem Bixby's land.

The half-breeds must have known who incited Indian Pete. There could be no other reason for murdering them. Someone feared what the dead men might have told. Whoever that person was, he would benefit if Dick Collins failed in his enterprise.

This fact seemed to put Abe Geesel in the clear. Clayton was the one who could secure the land if Dick didn't take up his option.

Roy decided to think things through a little farther, and then investigate by himself.

CHAPTER TWELVE

THE MYSTERIOUS MR. CLAYTON

It was nearly two o'clock when Roy Rogers left the jail with Dick and Gimlet. Eight hours had passed since breakfast and all three men were hungry. They headed for the Gopher Creek restaurant where a good meal was guaranteed for less than a dollar, and found a table near the large front window with gold-leaf lettering. The place was cool and clean and the table was spread with a snow-white cloth.

In the course of the meal Dick told Gimlet about his talk with Abe Geesel. The old man's reaction was typical. He expressed his opinion of Geesel in a vitriolic manner, emphasizing his remarks with jabs of his fork.

"The fact remains," Dick said when Gimlet had finished, "we can't get any more cash for the job."

"We c'n do one o' two things then," replied Gimlet. "We c'n quit now an' hunt us up a couple o' jobs, or we c'n starve."

Roy knew that he might just as well be as penniless as his friends, for all the good his own cash would do. He didn't even suggest financing the remainder of the job, because he knew that, in accordance with the terms of the agreement, Dick couldn't accept his help.

"We won't starve," said Dick. "I've enough left to cover this meal, and before we leave I'll have enough to lay in a few supplies to keep us fed for the next two weeks."

"On credit?" asked Gimlet.

Dick shook his head and said, "Nope." Reaching into his pocket, he brought out a heavy gold watch. "My father's," he explained briefly. Opening the case with his thumbnail, he removed a small, circular piece of heavy paper which he looked at for a moment, then handed to Roy Rogers. "That's a picture of my mother," he said. "That's Tom when he was a baby, sittin' on her lap. I'm the wide-eyed kid standin' alongside."

Roy gazed at the picture of a fine-looking woman whose eyes had the same intelligent depths which had attracted him to Dick. "You look a lot like your mother," he told Dick, handing back the picture.

"Thanks." Dick tucked the picture in an old leather wallet from which he drew three one-dollar bills.

Roy said, "Let me buy the lunch, Dick."

Dick shook his head and Roy didn't argue the point. He knew Dick's pride had suffered a stunning blow during the interview with Geesel. He knew it would restore that pride in some measure, if Dick paid for the meal. Much as he disliked seeing his friend's last money handed over to the cashier of the restaurant, he felt that it was better that way.

Dick closed the case of his watch with a snap. "I've got an offer for the watch," he said. "We'll get cash enough for food."

"Look here, Dick," said Roy Rogers. "Let's face things squarely."

"What d'you mean, Roy?"

"You and I both know you can get that oil if you've half a chance. We both know that, if it weren't for that lopsided agreement Geesel drew up, you'd have no trouble at all in raising the capital you need. Let me buy your watch for enough to finish the job."

Dick shook his head slowly. "Thanks, Roy," he said. "I can't sell it to you."

"Why not?"

"In the first place, you don't need a watch. You'd buy it to help me out, not because you wanted it. You'd buy it, and then some day after this oil experiment's finished, one way or the other, you'd send the watch to me as a present. I don't want that. In the second place, if Geesel found that I got cash from you, he'd find some way to call it a violation of the contract. Maybe the law wouldn't back him up in the long run, but he'd find some way to tie our hands so we couldn't work the well."

Roy understood Dick's attitude about the gift. He remembered days in his own life when his pride had been a lot bigger than his bankroll. He probably would have felt as Dick did, under similar conditions.

"I can sell the watch to Skinny Yates."

"The barkeep in the Silver Dollar?" queried Gimlet.

"Yes." Dick shoved back his plate. "While you two are eatin' your apple pie, I'll go over and see him."

"All right," said Roy. "We'll wait here for you."

"Don't you touch none o' the drinkables in there," warned Gimlet.

"Don't worry."

"Remember what one drink done tuh me," added the old man.

Dick stopped at the desk near the door long enough to pay for the three meals, then went out of the restaurant.

Through the window Roy watched Dick as he crossed the street and entered the Silver Dollar. Then he turned to Gimlet.

"What about Tom's horse and saddle?" he inquired.

"What about 'em?"

"They haven't been found yet, but they probably will turn up sooner or later. Can't they be sold for as much as you need to get your drills and tools?"

Gimlet made a wry face. "Roy," he said, "you don't know how flat busted we went tuh make up the payment on that doggoned option."

"Oh."

"Tom didn't own his horse or saddle. Neither does Dick an' neither do I. We couldn't get together all the cash Lem Bixby called for, so we throwed our hosses an' saddles an' just about all else we had, intuh the deal. Bixby was doggoned fine about it, too. He allowed us more'n the horses were worth an' told us we could keep usin' the critters fer as long as we wanted to."

"I see," replied Roy softly. "You fellows certainly staked everything on bringing in that oil well."

Gimlet nodded. "If we don't bring it in," he said, "we're licked bad! The worst of it is, I'll be the one to blame."

"You?"

Gimlet nodded. "It was my say-so that got Dick an' Tom to take up that land."

"Gimlet," said Roy, "I've a hunch about that deal."

"Yeah?"

"I think you fellows are going to have a bath in oil before another two weeks go by."

Gimlet sighed. His eye took on a dreamy look. "I seen it happen once," he said. "Years ago. I was workin' on a job an' when the oil come in, it just gushed up like water outen a hose. The boys that owned the well got soused from head tuh toe with the dirty black stuff, but how they loved it. It was like takin' a bath in jools an' gold. That's what it was."

When Dick returned he had a pitifully small amount of cash, but it was sufficient, with careful buying, to fill the saddlebags with staple foods to fend off starvation for the next two weeks.

"You two go on back to the job," Roy said when the things were packed on the horses. "I'll join you there later."

"I thought you was goin' back with us," said Gimlet.

"I have a few things to do while I'm in town," explained Roy. "I'll see you in camp."

Dick nodded without pressing the cowboy for further details. "Come on," he said to Gimlet. "If we hurry, we'll be able to get in a few hours of work."

Gimlet said, "All right," and climbed to the saddle.

Roy stood at Trigger's side and watched his friends ride away. He waved as they looked back, and called, "I'll see you."

He had no difficulty in finding the office of Luther Abercrombie, the Gopher Creek attorney. The lawyer's office was on the second floor of the building which housed the post office and bank.

It was a small but neat office and the lawyer was a small, neat man with well-kept hands and a small, clipped mustache.

"And what can I do for you?" he asked when Roy had taken a chair.

"I was talking to Lem Bixby a little while ago. I guess you know him, don't you, Abercrombie?"

"Oh, yes, yes, indeed!" replied the lawyer. "Lem and I go fishing together whenever I can sneak away from my work." He smiled. "Lem's great company."

"I suppose you already know I'm interested in the Bixby land."

"News gets around fast in Gopher Creek," grinned the lawyer. "I heard that you were going to give Dick Collins a hand. I'm glad of it. I'd like to see him make good."

"He has a tough proposition," said Roy.

"I know it. I've seen the contract Geesel drew up and it's one of the most unusual documents I've read."

"Is it legal?"

"It would stand up in any court," replied Abercrombie. "I went through it very carefully to find some loophole, but there was none. Geesel has Collins right under his thumb. From what I've heard, he's going to make Dick stop working on the well."

"He won't stop working until his option expires."

"Can he keep going?"

"He'll keep going somehow," replied Roy.

Abercrombie said, "I hope so." He offered a box to Roy, asking, "Cigar?"

Roy shook his head and declined with thanks.

Abercrombie lighted a cigar with meticulous care and then said, "You came here for some reason, Mr. Rogers. What can I do for you?"

"Bixby told me there was a second option on the land we've just been discussing. He said the option had been handled by you."

Abercrombie nodded.

"Do you mind telling me who Mr. Clayton is?"

"I'd be glad to tell you," replied the lawyer, "but the truth is, I know very little about him. In fact, I've never seen the man."

"You haven't?"

"No. He's in the oil business in a town some distance east of Gopher Creek, a place called Osage. He wrote, saying my name had been given him by an acquaintance. He asked me to investigate the property Lem Bixby owned. I replied, giving full details about the deal with Collins."

Roy nodded.

Abercrombie studied the end of his cigar for a moment. "Several weeks went by," he continued, "before I heard from Clayton again. This time he asked me to see if I could get a second option on the land, one that would take effect if Collins failed to take up his first option. I discussed it with Bixby and a price was agreed upon. Clayton sent his check in payment and the deal was closed. That's all there is to it."

"You say he's in Osage?"

Abercrombie nodded.

"He'd have no claim at all, if Collins took up the first option, would he?"

"None whatsoever. I warned him that he might be throwing his money away, but he seemed willing to take the risk."

"It would certainly be to his interest to keep Dick from getting oil, wouldn't it?"

Abercrombie nodded with a trace of a smile. "You're driving at something," he said. "It might be worth investigating further."

"You wouldn't know Clayton if you saw him, eh?"

"No."

Roy rose from the chair and put out his hand. "Thanks," he said.

Luther Abercrombie shook hands and once more made a pointed remark. "If I learn of anyone in town who's friendly with Clayton, I'll let you know. I suppose I can reach you at Collins's camp, eh?"

"If I'm not there," replied Roy, "leave word for me."

As Roy Rogers left the lawyer's office he felt that

in Luther Abercrombie, as in Lem Bixby, Dick Collins and Gimlet had a friend who was pulling for them to make good. How simple their problem would be, with so many friends to help, if it weren't for the restricting clause in Abe Geesel's contract! Bixby would have welcomed the chance to help, financially or otherwise. So would Abercrombie. Roy was sure of it.

He reached the ground floor and paused to look at the man who had just turned in at the entrance to Abe Geesel's office. He was struck by the shifty-eyed, unpleasant appearance of Snag Pritchard.

CHAPTER THIRTEEN

CROOKS MEET

Abe Geesel poured cloudy, black coffee into a thick, cracked cup that had no handle. He added a few drops of thick, condensed milk from a can, then stirred the mixture slowly. He was seated at the table near the bed, uncertain whether to feel jubilant or morose. He had learned that the three half-breeds were dead, and he knew why. He knew who had killed them. Geesel was glad they were dead, but he was depressed by the knowledge that he would have to tap his hoarded wealth to pay the killer for his work.

There was a rap on the door. Geesel muttered, "He isn't wasting any time," then audibly called, "Come in."

Snag Pritchard entered the room and closed the door behind him. "Bolt the door," said Geesel. Snag nodded and slid the heavy bolt across the groove.

"If you want a cup of coffee," Geesel said with rare hospitality, "rinse out that other cup and pour yourself some."

"No, thanks," replied Pritchard. "None of that stuff you brew." He strode over to the cot and sat down on the dirty, ragged blanket. "You've probably heard the news," he said.

"You muffed the job," replied the moneylender. He sipped noisily from the cup. "You muffed it," he repeated, looking at Snag Pritchard.

Snag scowled darkly. "Just what d'you mean by that? You wanted three hombres put where they couldn't talk. I put 'em there. That's what you wanted, ain't it?"

"The frame-up didn't work out though, did it?"

"What frame-up?"

Geesel placed his cup on the table, wiped his mouth with the back of his hand, crossed his legs and turned to face Pritchard directly. "Do you," he said, "think I'm an utter fool? You know what frame-up I'm talking about. You tried to frame Gimlet for the murder. It didn't work out that way."

"There wasn't nothin' said in our agreement about framin' someone else for the job. That was my own idea."

"You bungled it."

Snag Pritchard was on his feet. "Listen tuh me, Geesel," he said hotly. "If you're tryin' to get out of payin' off for that job, you'd better think again." He tapped the gun on his belt significantly. "I did all I agreed tuh do an' I expect to be paid off in hard cash. What's more, I expect to be paid off right now. That's the reason I'm here."

"You'll get your money," replied Geesel. "I'm not

one to back out of an agreement. I was simply stating that you hadn't done as neat a job as you might have. I don't like bungled jobs. They're dangerous! You'd have been better off if you hadn't tried to add the fancy touches. All you succeeded in doing was to make Collins and Gimlet, and this new friend of theirs, all the more determined to find the man who killed the half-breeds."

"You just pay me, and never mind the lecture," growled Snag. "If you don't like the way I do things, find someone else to do your dirty work."

"Stay right there on the cot," said Geesel, rising from the chair and walking to the safe. "I'll get your money."

"I'll stay here," said Snag Pritchard.

Geesel squatted before the safe and placed one hand on the dial. He looked toward Pritchard, then shifted his body so the killer couldn't see the combination as it was worked.

Pritchard, seeing the other man's cautious movements, grinned in a twisted, sneering way and said, "Don't be afraid I'll try tuh see the combination to that can. I ain't here to rob yuh, Geesel. All I want is what I earn."

Geesel worked the combination slowly. Three turns to the right, to a certain number, then one turn to the left, two turns to the right stopping at number seventeen. He grasped the handle of the safe

"I Ain't Here to Rob Yuh, Geesel," Sneered Snag

and pulled down, then the door swung open. He glanced at Pritchard again, and saw that the long-toothed man was leaning back, blowing cigarette smoke upward, forming rings that drifted to the ceiling.

Abe Geesel took two thin, flat keys from his vest pocket. With one of these he unlocked an inner compartment in the safe and drew out a tin cash-box. He placed this on the floor and opened it with the second of the keys. Carefully he counted out ten bills of ten dollars each. Then he locked the box and replaced it. He locked the inner compartment, then closed the safe's door and spun the dial to lock it.

The voice of Snag Pritchard had an amused ring when he spoke. "You ain't so smart, Geesel. What you should've done, was get that cash out before I came an' have it handy so's you wouldn't have tuh open the safe. It would've been a cinch fer me to plug you in the back with a bullet or stick you with a knife while the safe was open."

The moneylender made no reply to this. He sat down at his desk and jerked at the warped drawer. It stuck, and he had to wriggle it sideways a few times before he could get it open. He drew out a carefully written document and laid it on the desk. He dipped the pen in ink and held it toward Snag Pritchard. "Here," he said. "Sign this receipt and the cash is yours."

Snag Pritchard's brow darkened. "Nothin' was said about my signin' any papers," he grumbled. "Lemme see that thing you call a receipt."

Geesel nodded. "Go ahead and read it."

The document was short and to the point. Snag caught its significance at a glance, and objected strenuously. "I won't sign any paper like that!" he snapped. "That's a confession of murder!"

"Not exactly."

"It says that you've paid me one hundred dollars for shootin' the three half-breeds, an' it gives the date, the time an' place. If that ain't a murder confession, I don't know what is!"

"I," said Geesel, "call it 'Life Insurance,' or, if you prefer, 'Double Cross Insurance.'"

"You must think I'm loco!"

Geesel shook his head slowly and showed a faint trace of a smile. "I don't think you're loco, Pritchard," he said. "If that document fell into the wrong hands it would implicate me, because I'm the one who pays you, just as deeply as you. For that reason you may be quite sure I won't let anyone see the confession. It is simply to make sure you don't try to frame *me* for the murder. You might be more successful in your next attempt at a frame-up." He counted the bills in his hand. "The hundred dollars is waiting, Pritchard."

Snag saw the truth of Geesel's statement. The document would certainly be as dangerous to Geesel as it would to himself. "Gimme that pen," he growled.

Geesel dipped the pen in ink again and handed it to Pritchard, who affixed his name on the line provided for the purpose.

"There!" he said, laying down the pen. "Pay me!"

Geesel glanced at the signature, folded the paper and put it back in his desk. Then he counted out the money, slowly and carefully, and shoved the small pile toward Snag Pritchard.

"Now," he said, "I want to talk to you about another proposition."

"Now," replied the killer, "I'm ready to talk. Who else d'you want killed?"

"I don't want anyone killed. That is, not necessarily. Indian Pete didn't do as thorough a job as I had hoped he would. Collins isn't yet ready to give up."

"Redheads don't quit easy," commented the yellow-toothed man.

"He still has a couple of weeks to bring in the oil. He's got some friend who just arrived to help him and there's a chance—a slim one, I admit, but nevertheless a *chance*—that he might be successful. I don't want him to be."

"Then you want me to shoot him?"

"No. I have a better plan, Pritchard. If Collins were murdered there would be more investigation and it might turn a spotlight on me."

"What's your plan?"

"You ride out to Collins's camp and offer to help bring in the well. You can win the confidence of Collins and Gimlet by telling some story about me. Let them think you want to get even with me for something I've done to you. You can offer to work for nothing, just to put one over on me."

"Me work fer nothin'?"

"I'll pay you."

"But look here, I don't want money so bad that I'm willin' to work for it!"

"Don't be a fool. You won't have to work hard. Just be on the job and do whatever is necessary to make sure the well doesn't start giving oil. You will soon learn of some way to sabotage the work and make it appear to be an accident. When the first of the month arrives, and the option lapses, I'll pay you off and I'll pay you well!"

"How much?" asked Snag practically.

"We'll talk about that later."

"We'll talk about it right now, Geesel. I'll do what yuh want, but it'll cost the same as it would if I had tuh rub out those gents. One hundred dollars!"

"Very well," replied Abe Geesel.

A few moments later, Snag Pritchard left the office

with a crafty smile on his wolflike face. He had thought of a way to earn the money without spending more than a few hours at the oil well. "Nothin' was said," he told himself, "about Dick Collins gettin' killed in an 'accident.'"

CHAPTER FOURTEEN

After his conference with Luther Abercrombie, during which he learned that the mysterious Mr. Clayton, who held the second option on Lem Bixby's land, lived in Osage, Roy Rogers decided to visit that community. Time was a factor. Because of this, much as he disliked riding away on the trip without advising Dick and Gimlet that he wouldn't join them in camp as early as they might expect him, he had no choice. He started for Osage soon after he noticed Snag Pritchard entering Abe Geesel's office.

Sunset found Trigger loping across open country. The palomino seemed glad to be on the move. A cool breeze came up after the sun went down and Roy thought of Dick and Gimlet, with their meager equipment and scanty protection against the weather. The fact that he, himself, might be uncomfortable without the poncho and other things he had lent them, never entered his head. Just before darkness closed in, Roy reined up near a stream. He pulled on a windbreaker, filled his canteen, and gave Trigger a chance to drink the refreshing water. There were miles of riding ahead,

129

some of them through hilly country. It was these hills that made the trip by horseback considerably shorter than it would have been in an automobile following the devious twisting and turning of the rutted wagon road that wove in and out through the innumerable valleys.

Roy followed a direct line as closely as possible. He gave Trigger his head and then relaxed the reins. He was heading for Osage to learn all he could about Mr. Clayton. He hoped to find some way to connect the would-be purchaser of Bixby's land with the murder of the half-breeds, and indirectly with the murder of Dick's brother, Tom. It was a job to be done in person. He couldn't make a satisfactory inquiry by telephone.

As he rode, Roy summarized the situation, filing the assorted facts in an orderly arrangement in his mind. There was no doubt about the fact that Indian Pete and his friends had murdered Tom. Roy hadn't even handed the note of warning with Pete's signature to the sheriff so that it might be examined for fingerprints. Roy accepted Pete as Tom's killer without question. But someone, obviously, had incited the half-breeds. The three prisoners had been killed so they couldn't name that person.

The man who killed the half-breeds had tried to frame Gimlet. This had involved giving Gimlet a drugged drink, which meant that the killer had to

be in the Silver Dollar. There had been no strangers
there, according to what Roy had learned, so the
killer must be someone who was known in Gopher
Creek.

Roy set these facts aside and considered the situation from another angle.

There was a fortune in oil on Lem Bixby's land.
Dick Collins was close to getting it. If he succeeded,
Abe Geesel would have a one-quarter interest in
the property. If he failed, Geesel would have nothing. Why, then, was Geesel contributing to Dick's
failure?

Did Geesel sincerely think that there was no use
in risking another hundred dollars? That was hard
to believe. On the surface it seemed that Geesel
could in no way benefit if Dick's option were not
taken up. Clayton was the one who would benefit.
Clayton would be able to buy the Bixby property,
and with it, all that Dick, Gimlet and Tom had done.

Roy decided that he needed the answers to a few
specific questions. Did Clayton have an accomplice
in Gopher Creek, and, if so, who was helping him?
Roy felt sure that with the answer to these points
he would know who murdered the half-breeds. The
next question concerned Abe Geesel. Why was he
unwilling to give Dick Collins further help? More
than this, why was he unwilling to let Dick have
help from *any* source?

The answer to one of these questions might be found in the town of Osage.

Roy figured that he could hardly reach Osage before midnight. That would mean that he'd be unable to make inquiries until the next moring. If he had good luck, he might join Dick and Gimlet around sundown. He didn't know that a murderer would be waiting, gun cocked, to ambush him on that return trail!

It had been a cold night, and the morning was gray and cheerless, when Dick and Gimlet wakened in the insufficient shelter of the lean-to. Dick swung his arms and slapped his sides to take the chill out of his body, while Gimlet waved his hat at a few sparks and a pile of dry wood, coaxing life into the campfire. The old man was in a dour mood.

"I knew," he grumbled, "that it was too good tuh be true! We ain't goin' tuh git no help from that friend o' yores."

"Do you mean Roy Rogers?"

"That's who I mean," replied Gimlet. He slapped his hat on his head and got down on his knees to blow gustily at the fire. "He was tuh join us here yesterday. Wal, I didn't see nothin' of him."

"He didn't say he'd join us yesterday. He said he'd join us. He didn't say when."

"Humph. The way he talked, I thought he meant

yesterday. Anyhow, he ain't here."

"After all, you ungrateful old galoot," said Dick with a grin, "there's no reason why he should help us. He's already done a lot more than we had any reason to expect."

"Disappointin' me like this," growled Gimlet.

"You'll feel better after you've got some food under your belt. Move over and let me get the skillet and coffee pot balanced on the fire."

Gimlet was surly as he munched his food. Dick used up more of the supplies than he had planned, but he thought a substantial meal was needed after the cold night. He'd skimp on the noonday meal to keep the rationing in balance. As Gimlet filled his plate with fried ham and potatoes for the third time, he glanced at Dick and saw the grin on the younger man's face.

"Feel better now?" asked Dick.

"Why should I?"

"They say a good meal always helps a man's disposition. I hoped your mood had improved, you ornery old catamount."

"Roy's cookin' was better," grumbled Gimlet.

Dick couldn't suppress a laugh. "You," he said, "are the most cussed old man I've ever known. Isn't there anything that could make you happy?"

"Sure there is," snapped Gimlet.

"Well, for heaven's sake, tell me what it is!"

"I'd like tuh git soused from head tuh foot with oil gushin' out of the ground from a well I own! That's what'd make me happy."

"I see," replied Dick more soberly.

"Yes, siree! I'd just scrunch down on the ground an' it'd be two inches deep in oil, an' I'd waller around in it, an' I'd slap it with my hands an' kick it with my feet, an' all the time I'd know that it was mine, an' that it was worth so much a bar'l, an' that I was goin' tuh be rich! I'd know that I c'd buy the food I liked, an' go where I pleased! I'd know that I could buy me a pair o' boots that didn't pinch my feet. Two pair, dagnab it! Not one pair o' boots, but *two* pair! Maybe a *dozen* pair! Money wouldn't matter!"

Gimlet had risen during his exclamation-studded dream. Now he resumed his seat near the fire and took a big gulp of black coffee.

"Another thing," he finished, "I'd have fresh cream in my coffee."

The meal was finished and the few plates and the skillet scrubbed clean. The sun slanted its beams from the eastern horizon and the chill began to leave the air. It was then that Gimlet saw a horseman approaching the camp.

"I know that critter," he told Dick as the rider drew near.

"Who is he?"

"His name's Snag Pritchard. I seen him yesterday in the Silver Dollar."

"I wonder," said Dick, "why he's coming here?"

"I dunno," replied Gimlet. "He generally hangs around town, pickin' up what cash he can by playin' gamblin' games in the back room of the café."

Pritchard dismounted at the fire.

CHAPTER FIFTEEN

CRASH OF DOOM

Snag Pritchard accepted Dick's invitation and poured himself a cup of coffee from the pot which had been kept warm by the fire. "I heard a lot about your trip to town," he began. "Gimlet had a pretty narrow escape, didn't he?"

Dick nodded, but Gimlet said, "I didn't! I warn't in no danger at any time. I knowed all along that I could prove I didn't have no part in the murder of them breeds."

Snag said, "O.K. Let it pass."

"Why'd you come here?" demanded Gimlet.

"I wanted to have a talk with you two gents. I started early so I could get here before you got goin' on your day's work. I didn't want to interrupt you." Pritchard took a sip of coffee. "Geesel," he said, "wouldn't help you, eh?"

Dick shook his head.

"Do you think you can do the job without his help?"

"We're going to try mighty hard."

"That's the stuff," said Snag Pritchard approvingly. "I sure would like to see you put one over on him."

"How can we do that?" asked Gimlet.

"By bringin' in the well!"

"That means he's due tuh make a profit on the deal. How'd that put anything over on him?"

Snag shrugged his shoulders. "I don't know," he said, "but doesn't it seem to you as if he don't *want* you to bring it in?"

Dick agreed that this appeared to be the case.

"You ain't told us why you come here," snapped Gimlet. "If you got somethin' to say, say it an' be done with it. We got a lot of work tuh do."

Snag Pritchard took on a confidential manner. "I'll tell you why I'm here," he said slowly. "I'm here because I'm in the same boat as you two."

"What d'yuh mean by that?"

"I've got cause to hate Abe Geesel."

"You?"

Snag nodded.

"Who," demanded Gimlet, "says that we hate Abe Geesel?"

"If you don't, you should. He's hogtied you two with the most unfair agreement that's ever been drawn up. It wouldn't hurt him to let you have a little more cash, or if he don't want to do it, he could let you borrow a few bucks from someone else. He's simply tryin' to keep you from success. That's all!"

"What are you getting at?" asked Dick. He didn't

particularly dislike Pritchard, even though he wasn't friendly with the man. It was simply a case of being disinterested.

"I'll tell you what I'm getting at," replied Pritchard. "I want to square an old account with Abe Geesel! I want to even things up."

"What's he ever done tuh you?" asked Gimlet.

"He swindled me out of a lot of money with a crooked deal. I can't prove it's crooked, but it was!"

"Bah!" spat Gimlet. "You never had no money to be swindled out of."

"Have you got any money?" retorted Pritchard. "Not a red cent," he said, answering his own question. "But if you don't get the oil, wouldn't you say it was because of Abe Geesel? Sure you would! He's the one that's goin' tuh swindle you out of a pile of money with a doggoned unfair agreement. He took me the same way!"

"You know a lot about our business," said Dick.

"So does everyone in Gopher Creek! It's all over town the way Geesel turned you away yesterday!"

Dick's cheeks burned at the recollection of his humiliation.

"You peddled your watch to the barkeep in the Silver Dollar so you could eat! If that ain't reachin' bottom, what is?"

Dick nodded grimly.

"Geesel is laughin' all over the place at the way

you two have worked and slaved here to bring in oil, and he knows darn well you ain't goin' tuh be able tuh do it!"

"Where can he gain anything if we don't?"

"Ain't yuh figured that out? That's easy! They's some other gent that's got an option an' he's probably offered Geesel a cut in his share if you gents don't make out. A bigger cut than Geesel will get with you."

Dick nodded. This seemed a logical explanation. But what lay back of it? Did it mean that Geesel had been responsible for the murders? For Tom's death, as well as the half-breeds'?

"I'm here," continued Snag Pritchard, "to see if you'll let me work along with you. You need someone to take the place of your brother. I'm a good worker and I'd admire the chance to work against Abe Geesel."

"When you said we were flat broke, you hit the nail on the head. I can't pay for any help."

"Who said anything about pay?"

"Yuh mean yuh want tuh work fer free?" asked Gimlet.

"I'll get paid enough by seein' Geesel squirm!"

Dick felt that there was more to Pritchard's desire to work than appeared on the surface. He couldn't put his finger on anything tangible, but a feeling of distrust gnawed at his subconscious mind and warned him to have nothing to do with the lean-faced man with jaws and teeth like those of a wolf. Yet, there was no reason to refuse the help Pritchard offered. Help was needed, desperately needed.

Gimlet eyed the store of supplies appraisingly. As if Snag Pritchard knew what went through the old man's mind, he said, "I've got some grub in my saddlebags. You needn't worry about that."

The furrows of concern smoothed away from Gimlet's brow.

Dick said, "There's nothing in the agreement with Geesel that says we can't let someone work here. If you're on the level, Pritchard, and willing to take a chance along with us, you've got a job."

"That's all I asked for," replied Snag Pritchard with what he thought was a pleasant smile. "Let's see what the job looks like."

Dick showed Pritchard the derrick and pointed out the various parts. He showed how the plummet and the windlass were used and explained the operation of the small wood-engine that supplied steam power.

"I've never worked on a job like this," Snag said. "But I'll do what I'm told and help in any way I can."

Dick nodded. He showed Pritchard the tool house and the small watertight box in which explosives were stored.

"What are the explosives for?" asked Snag.

"In a day or so, when we've drilled down a little farther, we'll torpedo the shaft. That means we'll fire off some charges underground and see if that will start the oil flowing."

Snag nodded. He wasn't concerned with what happened in a day or so. It wasn't likely he'd be on the job that long. With any sort of luck, he calculated, he would be through some time before noon.

"Our main worry right now," said Dick, "is drills. They wear down and get dull mighty fast when they're cuttin' through hard rock. It's a job keepin' them sharp."

"Do you need more drills?"

"We sure could use them! We're down to the last drill. If it breaks off down in the shaft, it might take days to fish it out. Gimlet handles all of the drilling himself. We've got to be mighty careful."

Snag smiled inwardly. If nothing else offered itself as a chance to sabotage the job, there might be a way to snap the drill while it was in the shaft. He stored this bit of information in a recess of his mind.

They stood at the base of the derrick which towered to an apex high overhead. Snag noticed the windlass, around which ran a heavy rope with many splices. This ran from the windlass to a pulley at the top of the derrick, then down to a cylindrical piece of equipment called the "bailer."

The bailer was lowered into the shaft to draw up crushed rock, dirt and water as the drilling progressed. Its weight was close to three hundred pounds and it hung, suspended, overhead.

Snag noticed that the rope had already snapped many times. The splices testified to that. Now if that bailer happened to fall, if it landed on Dick Collins, the result would undoubtedly be fatal. Work on the oil well would be stopped effectively and permanently. Why bother to spend time and energy working on the job when it wasn't necessary?

Snag recalled what Geesel had said. He didn't want Dick murdered, because there would be too much of an investigation. Well, if Dick were to die as the result of an accident—that would be a different matter.

As Snag Pritchard thought of these things, his hand surreptiously fingered the knife in his side pocket. He studied the heavy rope that was dark with age. He drew the knife and opened the largest blade. He didn't hear what Dick was saying.

Dick had been outlining the procedure of oil drilling. His talk concerning rigs, stems, bits and walking beams was entirely lost on Snag, whose

Snag Didn't Hear What Dick Was Saying

mind was filled with murder. "You can see," said Dick, "there's not much to the job." He turned to look at Snag as he spoke. This brought Snag back to the conversation.

"Now I'll explain the drill," said Dick.

Pritchard, merely to have something to say, asked, "How does the drill fasten to the upper part?"

"I'll show you." Dick stooped to unscrew the V-shaped drill. Snag grew tense. Dick was just where the killer wanted him to be, directly beneath the suspended bailer. Snag measured distances in his mind. He didn't want to make a mistake. He held the knife in readiness and moved back half a step to be nearer the windlass. He glanced toward Gimlet, occupied with the horses in the corral.

The moment had come. Snag's arm moved carefully, the keen edge of his knife touched the halfrotten cable and bit in.

The best plans sometimes fail because of some small stumbling block against which no amount of foresight could have guarded. Snag Pritchard's quickly improvised scheme for murdering Dick Collins failed in part because of a drop of oil.

For lack of a bit of oil the rusty pulley near the apex of the derrick had a rasping squeak.

At the instant the rope parted and the bailer

began its drop, the pulley emitted a frightful squeak which caught Gimlet's attention. The old man yelled, but Dick had already leaped back impulsively. Snag, seeing Dick's leap from the path of the down-coming bailer, shouted a warning, then shoved.

Dick had been out of harm's way. Snag's sudden push sent him back toward the point of peril. The pulley's high-pitched scream grew louder as the bailer gathered speed. Gimlet saw what was happening and found himself unable to move or speak. He was frozen, riveted to the spot near the corral, and could only stare at the impending disaster. As Dick stumbled forward he tried to throw himself to one side, and he threw up his hands and arms to protect his head. This was a futile effort—nothing like the strength of man could break the fall of that heavy bailer. It crashed down, brushing Dick's arm, glancing on his shoulder, and smashing through the planks of the derrick's floor.

Dick staggered, clutched at air, and fell in a crumpled heap upon the platform while blood ran from ugly gashes to form an ever-increasing pool on the floor.

Gimlet came up on the run. By the time he reached the scene of tragedy, Snag Pritchard was bent over the motionless form of Dick Collins.

"Is he kilt?" yelled Gimlet.

"I don't think so," replied Snag. "He's breathing."

"I seen it happen!" exclaimed the old man. "I seen it fallin', an' there wasn't nothin' I could do about it."

Snag cursed himself for Gimlet's benefit. "It was all my fault," he complained bitterly. "I tried to shove him out of the way, but just as I did it, he jumped back! We were workin' against each other! If I hadn't shoved him, he'd have been in the clear."

"Tain't yore fault," replied Gimlet generously. "I seen the hull thing happen. You tried tuh save him, but he jumped back, like you said."

Gimlet was bent over Dick, tearing away the remains of his shirt to examine the ugly wounds. "Git some water," he commanded.

"Dick, Dick," pleaded Gimlet, when Snag had gone for water. "Yuh gotta pull through this, Dick. Yuh jest gotta." He whipped out his bandanna and tried to staunch the flow of blood.

Snag took ample time in going for the water. He hadn't been wholly successful, but he was satisfied. Gimlet would confirm his story about an accident and Dick was just as surely helpless to go on working as he would have been had the bailer's fall been fatal.

Yes, Snag was satisfied with his work.

CHAPTER SIXTEEN

DRY-GULCH PLANS

Snag Pritchard's horse was badly winded and soaking wet with sweat as the rider pulled to a cruelly sudden halt before the sheriff's office. Snag's inward jubilation was belied by the expression of worry and deep concern he wore. He leaped to the ground and strode to Jim Lambert's office. As he burst through the door he felt an instant's misgiving. Skinny Yates, the bartender from the Silver Dollar, was seated at one end of the sheriff's desk.

"There's another," cried Skinny as he saw Snag Pritchard. "Snag Pritchard. Put his name down."

"What about me?" demanded Snag.

"The sheriff is workin' on the murder o' them half-breeds," Skinny Yates explained.

Snag saw the sheriff writing his name at the bottom of a list of ten or more names. "If you suspect me—" he sputtered angrily.

"Naw, nothin' like that," replied the bartender in a calming voice. "We're only tryin' tuh make up a list of everyone who was in the café while Gimlet was in there yesterday. You were there, Snag. Don't yuh remember?"

"Of course, I was. What's that got to do with

the half-breeds?"

"It might have a lot to do with the murders," put
in Jim Lambert. "The killer tried to frame Gimlet.
To do that he put somethin' in his drink to make
him sleep. The killer of the prisoners was in the
café while Gimlet was there." He shoved the list
over to Skinny. "Look that list over an' tell me if
I've left anyone out," he said.

Skinny Yates took the list.

Jim Lambert looked up at Snag Pritchard and
said, "What do you want?"

Snag quickly resumed his studied expression of
worry and concern. "It's about Dick Collins," he
said. "He's had an accident out at his camp. I came
here on the run to get the doctor. D'you know
where he is, Sheriff?"

"You say Dick's had an accident?"

Snag nodded vigorously. "A bad one."

"What happened?"

"It's on account of the no-account equipment he's
usin' on that job, Sheriff. There was some kind of
heavy gadget, I think it's called the bailer, that's
hung from the top of the derrick on a half-inch rope.
The rope was old an' rotten. It snapped an' the
bailer hit Dick."

"The bailer!" exclaimed the sheriff. "You don't
want the doctor, you want the coroner!"

"Oh, it didn't hit him square," explained Snag.

"It sort of glanced off his shoulder. He's alive, but he's hurt mighty bad. Gimlet is there with him."

"Did you look in Doc Martin's office?"

"Nope. I came here first, because I thought you'd know if the Doc was in his office."

"I don't know whether he is or not. The coroner left here an hour ago to go after the body of Dick's kid brother. He took a couple of men with him. I don't know whether Doc Martin went along or not."

"I'll see if he's in his office," replied Snag.

"Hold on, Pritchard!"

Snag paused with the door half opened.

"What were you doin' at Collins's camp?"

"Why? Ain't I got a right to be there?"

"Answer my question!"

"Why, I—I just went there to see if I could help Dick an' Gimlet."

Jim Lambert squinted, disbelief stamped on his face. "You mean," he said slowly, "you went there to *work?*"

"Sure!"

"You knew Collins couldn't pay anyone for workin', didn't you?"

Snag nodded.

"Then why did you go there? Don't lie tuh me, Pritchard. You never done anything to help anyone in your life. You never *worked* that I know of.

It don't make sense for you to go and work on something hard, like the Collins job, unless you're paid plenty for it! Now let's have the true facts."

Snag gave Jim Lambert a story which was substantially the same as the one he had told Dick and Gimlet. Because he had rehearsed it thoroughly he managed to make it sound convincing. It was easy to register loathing and hatred when he spoke of Abe Geesel.

"All right," the sheriff said when Snag had finished. "Hurry over to Doc Martin's office. If you don't find him there, come back and I'll see if I can locate him."

Snag lost no time in getting away from there. He didn't like the listing of his name among the others who had been in the Silver Dollar, but reflecting on this as he hurried to the doctor's office, he realized that there was nothing to tie him to the shooting.

He was under no more suspicion than anyone else who had been in the café during Gimlet's visit. Though the sheriff might question all those who were on his newly compiled list, it was unlikely that anyone would be able to tell how Snag Pritchard had put a few grains of white powder in a drink he shoved toward Gimlet. Snag had been careful to remain in the background in the Silver Dollar. He reassured himself by recalling that Skinny Yates didn't even think of him until all the others had been listed.

He reached Doctor Martin's office to find Luther Abercrombie seated in the waiting room. The lawyer's greeting was agreeable, but not friendly. He invited Snag to sit beside him until the doctor had finished with a patient in the other room. Snag told about the accident at the derrick and found Abercrombie unusually interested.

"Are you sure it was an accident?" asked the lawyer.

"It must've been. I don't see how else it could've happened. Do you?"

The lawyer shook his head slowly and said, "I don't know what to think. There's something going on, and I can't find out what it is."

"Is that so?" replied Snag innocently, with a lifted eyebrow.

"A man named Rogers came to my office yesterday. He asked a lot of questions about the Collins camp. Prior to seeing me, he had called on Lem Bixby and questioned him."

"You don't say?"

"You probably knew that a man in Osage by the name of Clayton holds a second option on the land."

"I heard somethin' about it," replied Pritchard.

"A few minutes ago," the lawyer went on, "I had

a telephone call from Mr. Clayton. He seemed quite upset and wanted to know what was going on at the Collins camp."

Snag was all attention now. He tried to keep his voice casual. "Is that so?" he said.

"Yes. Rogers was in Osage early this morning, making inquiries about Clayton."

"Rogers? You mean Dick Collins's friend?"

"Of course!"

"He was in Osage?"

"Yes. He must have ridden over there last night."

"I wonder if he's still there?"

"No. He had left when Clayton phoned me. I think he's on the way to Collins's camp."

Snag had to get to Abe Geesel with this piece of news. He lighted a cigarette and tried to smoke it slowly. He didn't want Luther Abercrombie to think his departure sudden, and above all, he didn't want the lawyer to think it had anything to do with the information about Roy Rogers. He snubbed out the cigarette and looked at the clock on the wall. "Look, Mr. Abercrombie," he said, "there's no use of my stayin' around here. I've got a few things to do. You c'n tell Doc Martin about the accident at Collins's camp, can't you?"

"Of course," replied the lawyer affably.

"Tell him he should get out there as soon as he can."

"I will."

Snag left the office with a wave of his hand. He walked slowly until he was out of view from the office window, then he went as fast as possible to Abe Geesel's office.

Geesel listened attentively while Snag related what had happened at the derrick. He nodded a few times without comment. Then Snag told about Clayton's phone call to Luther Abercrombie. This brought the moneylender to his feet with an exclamation of anger.

"Who *is* this fellow Rogers?" he demanded. "Why is he snooping into other people's business?"

"How do I know?" asked Snag.

"Shut up! I'm not asking *you* questions." Geesel paced the floor, his hands clasped behind him. "If Rogers is smart, he'll be able to put two and two together and get the right answer," he muttered. "I wonder how much he found out about Clayton?"

Snag shrugged his shoulders without answering.

Geesel halted suddenly and turned toward his associate. "You say Rogers is on his way to Collins's camp right now?"

Snag was sulking after his last utterance had been thrown back at him. "Didn't say nothin'," he muttered. "I told you what Abercrombie said. That's all I know about it."

Geesel resumed his pacing. "On the way there

now," he mumbled, "traveling by horse." He went to his desk and pawed through a disorderly pile of papers until he found a map. This he spread out on the desk. "Come here," he said to Snag, without looking away from the map.

Snag moved to Geesel's side.

"Right here," said the moneylender, pointing with a pencil, "is the town of Osage. You've been there, haven't you?"

"Uh-huh," replied Snag. "A couple of times."

Geesel moved the pencil. He pointed to an area squared off with ink. "This," he said, "is the Bixby land."

"I oughtta know where that is. I don't need no map tuh show me."

"Right along here," Geesel went on, ignoring Snag's comment, "is the most direct route from Osage to the camp. If Rogers is going to the camp, he'll follow that route. It's an old Indian trail."

"What about it?"

"You're to meet him!"

"I am?"

"Yes. If you start now, you can find a good place somewhere along the trail. Hide there and wait for Rogers. Things have come to the point where we've got to take strong measures! We can't run any risks now."

"What'm I tuh do? Why should I hide an' wait

for Rogers?"

"You fool, you've got to shoot him! Why else would I send you out there?"

"Now hold on, Geesel. You're gettin' mighty free an' easy with the way you call on me tuh do things!"

"You'll be paid!"

"There's a matter of some money that's already due me."

"For what?"

"The job I already did at Collins's camp."

"That money doesn't come to you until the first of the month. How do I know Collins won't find some way to continue work on that well? I said I'd pay you the first of the month, if Collins didn't take up his option! That was the agreement."

"Is this to be another first-of-the-month proposition?" asked Snag.

"No. I'll pay you as soon as the job is done."

There was some haggling about a price, but an agreement was reached. Then Snag said, "Lemme see that map. I'll pick myself a place to wait."

A few minutes later Pritchard left the office on another mission of murder. This time, the victim was to be Roy Rogers!

CHAPTER SEVENTEEN

AMBUSHED

Roy Rogers left Osage earlier than he had planned. He had talked to several men he knew, and to others he had met in town and at Steve Logan's oil field. Steve Logan had proved to be an interesting character. He was one of the best oil men in that part of the country. Steve had spent most of his life prospecting and developing oil wells for other men. Finally he had acquired a piece of land in his own name and developed it until it was one of the best-paying wells in the vicinity. Steve Logan's name was highly respected by men in the business.

When Roy had mentioned Gimlet Lonergan, he had been surprised to learn that Logan and all those with him had the highest admiration for Gimlet's ability to spot oil-bearing land.

"If Gimlet says there's oil in the ground," Steve Logan had stated, "you can bet your bottom dollar it's there! That tough old wildcat's never been wrong in his life. He can spot oil land five miles away."

Logan had insisted on full details of Gimlet's present situation and Roy had given them.

Regarding John Clayton, Roy hadn't been able

to learn a great deal. Clayton had lived by himself
in the town of Osage for many years. He dabbled
in countless things, sticking at nothing long enough
to be successful. He was a man of nondescript appearance who might have been any age between
forty-five and sixty. At first he had been evasive, but
later had admitted purchasing a second option on
the Bixby land. He did so, he said, purely on the
strength of Gimlet's estimation of the property's
value.

Roy had wondered how Clayton knew about
Gimlet and Dick Collins when Steve Logan, who
had been Gimlet's partner at one time, knew nothing about the old man's present endeavor.

It also struck Roy as curious that John Clayton
had taken the risk of a second option. Clayton was
a conservative, mouse-like man, not at all the type
to gamble. Yet he had gambled heavily on Dick's
inability to bring in oil before the deadline.

Clayton had denied knowing anyone in Gopher
Creek. He had never heard, he said, of Abe Geesel.

Loping along the trail that would take him directly to Dick's camp without going through Gopher
Creek, Roy felt that his trip to Osage had proved
worth while, in spite of the meager facts he had concerning Clayton. Steve Logan had made the trip
worth while. Here, thought Roy, was another man
who would have been delighted to help Dick and

Gimlet, and Logan's help would have been of a substantial nature. If there were only some way to get around the restrictions of Geesel's contract! Apparently, though, there were none.

There had been a time when the trail was clearly defined and fairly open, but that had been in the days of Indian hunters and wild buffalo. Roy found it badly overgrown. Several times Trigger slowed and had to shove through thickets growing so close to the trail that they brushed Roy's legs and the palomino's sides.

During the first part of the trip, the sun had gleamed in Roy's eyes; then it beat down, hot, from directly overhead. After that it slanted against his back. Roy paused for water.

"In another hour," he told Trigger, stroking the silky neck of the palomino, "we'll be with Dick and Gimlet."

Men whose lives depend upon eternal vigilance are known to develop a peculiar sixth sense. Explorers in tropical jungles, hunters and trappers in the north woods, frontiersmen, plainsmen, woodsmen— all will verify this statement. Though psychologists cannot explain the phenomena, it is none the less true that the feeling of impending danger manifests itself in men like these. In some cases the warning comes in the form of a tingling of the scalp; other men may have a feeling of tension. In Roy's case, a

tiny vibration akin to an electric current passed up
and down his spine.

Roy hadn't known that sensation for some time,
but, as he prepared to mount for the last leg of his
journey, it was as if the touching of foot to stirrup
closed an electrical circuit. His spine tingled with
a warning of danger on the trail ahead. His face
sobered as he touched Trigger with his heels. He
couldn't imagine what peril might be lying in wait.
He tried to shake off the peculiar tingling. He tried
to tell himself it was nothing but imagination, or,
if not that, something that was caused by the long
and tiring ride. Instead of diminishing, as Roy rode
on toward Dick's camp the feeling of impending
trouble grew in intensity.

Roy knew all the signs and watched for them. His
keen eyes were in constant movement, covering the
trail ahead and beside him. He watched every copse
and shrub for the slightest movement. He was wary
as he approached every rock large enough to con-
ceal a man, and he tensed, ready for action, as he
passed an arroyo in which danger might be lurking.

He was within half an hour of camp when it happened. The trail at that point was on hard ground,
so strewn with rocks that there was little vegetation.
At one time a large stream had flowed parallel to
the trail, but this, through the years, had been re-
duced to a tiny trickle of water at the bottom of a

deep bed. The cowboy rode along the rim of the creek's bed with every sense alert. Then, though Roy gave no signal, Trigger halted abruptly, and stood stock-still like a good hunting dog coming to point.

"What's the matter with you, Trigger?" said Roy softly. "Why're we stopping here?"

The horse was frozen, his only movement an almost imperceptible trembling of the splendid muscles beneath the golden coat. Roy looked ahead. He studied both sides of the trail, the rocks on the left and the three-foot drop to the creek on the right. He saw nothing to cause Trigger's tension. Then he heard a click. It was the faintest of sounds, but it struck Roy's over-tensed nerves like a sledge-hammer blow on an anvil. It might have been the crack of the starter's pistol in a hundred-yard dash. Like runners poised at the starting line, Roy and Trigger exploded into action. The intelligent horse acted entirely without instruction. He leaped at the sound as if he knew attack to be the best defense. He leaped as if he knew, just as did Roy, why certain gunmen in the old west survived. It had always been a rule among those gunmen to take time to aim. Invariably they let the other fellow have the first shot, and it was always a hurried one and therefore inaccurate. The gunman fired second, but his shot didn't miss.

Trigger's leap, accompanied as it was by a wild, cowboy cry of defiance from Roy, made Snag Pritchard hurry his shot. The blast came directly ahead of, and slightly under, Roy and Trigger as they leaped into the gully. Roy had a fleeting glimpse of Snag Pritchard's face before his eyes riveted themselves to the long-barreled pistol. Roy's gun cleared leather while all four of Trigger's feet were off the ground. He slid his feet from the stirrups and dove through space toward Snag.

As Snag was bringing his gun around for a second shot, Roy's gun hand swung down in a short arc. The barrel of his weapon smashed against the knuckles of the killer's hand. Snag started a cry of surprise and pain, but it was choked back as the full weight and force of Roy's hard-muscled body struck. Both men sprawled on the ground.

Then Roy was on his feet, his hand gripping Pritchard's shirt. He jerked the disarmed dry-gulcher to his feet with one hand while he holstered his weapon with the other.

"We'll finish it with fists," Roy barked.

"Now wait," gasped Snag Pritchard, willing to try anything to gain an instant's time.

Roy's left shot out to jab Snag in the stomach. The killer gasped and began to double over. As his chin came down, Roy snapped his right in a sharp uppercut that landed flush on that descending chin. Snag's head jerked back with the force of the blow. His eyes were filmed and he was, at that moment, ready to drop, but Roy delivered one more blow to make certain. It was a smashing, full swing that began with his left hand low, and gathered force as he brought that hand around to crash perfectly at the side of Snag's chin.

Snag Pritchard was down, completely out.

"Now," muttered Roy, "there's something in which we can sink our teeth. When this fellow comes to, we'll ask a few questions, and we'll get some answers."

Grabbing Snag beneath the armpits, he dragged him to the creek. A little water splashed on the killer's face soon restored consciousness.

Snag's first words were, "Wha . . . what hit me?"

Roy filled Snag's hat with water and spilled it where it would do the most good. Snag came out of his stupor, sputtering and waving his arms.

"That'll do," said Roy. "You're not swimming."

Snag stopped squirming and looked at the young cowboy.

"Maybe you made a mistake," said Roy Rogers coolly. "Maybe you were gunning for someone else. On the other hand, you might have been looking for me for a reason that you'll explain. Do you want to talk now, or later?"

Snag Pritchard gazed at the speaker stupidly.

"Wha . . . What Hit Me?" Snag Muttered

"I—I—uh—I thought you were someone else," he mumbled.

"Who'd you think I was?" demanded Roy.

Snag mumbled a few words Roy couldn't catch.

"Who did you intend to dry-gulch?"

"I—I dunno his name—he—er—uh—" Snag was obviously groping for words.

Roy cut in sharply. "Who sent you to gun me?" he demanded.

The look of bewilderment left Snag's face, giving way to one of cunning. "I," he said, "won't talk."

Roy nodded briefly. "All right," he said. "We'll talk later." He drew Snag's gun and tossed it into the creek. Then, with the coil of lasso from his saddle, he deftly tossed a loop around Snag, who had gathered himself into a sitting position, and drew it tight. Snag's arms were held close to his sides.

Roy stood a few feet away and tossed additional coils of rope around his captive, throwing a double twist in each coil so it would stay in place. In a moment he was finished.

"Have you," he said, "got a horse?"

"I ain't talkin'," replied Snag Pritchard sullenly.

"Suits me," replied Roy as he tied the free end of the rope to the pommel of his saddle. "You can ride or walk, but you'll have the fastest walk you ever had." He prepared to mount.

Snag, envisioning what would happen, spoke quickly. "I've got a horse," he cried.

"Changed your mind about talking, eh?"

"I—I c-can't let yuh drag me."

Roy untied the rope from the pommel, ordered Snag to stand, then followed him while he got his horse from a near-by hiding place.

A moment later Roy was riding toward Dick's camp beside his prisoner. Now the sense of impending danger was gone.

CHAPTER EIGHTEEN

ROY MAKES PLANS

Gimlet ran to meet Roy as he approached camp. The old man was in a high state of excitement. When he saw Snag Pritchard, tied as a captive, his rage reached such a peak that for several minutes he could only howl imprecations and promise fifty-seven varieties of punishment. Roy, wondering what lay behind Gimlet's fury, dismounted and waited for the one-eyed man to calm down to reasoning level.

"I wanted tuh drill the half-breeds," Gimlet was shouting, "but I didn't do it. I left 'em for the law tuh deal with an' I found out there was a chance they might never o' hung. Wal, I ain't goin' tuh take no such a chance with this murderin', sneakin', double-crossin' polecat. I'm goin' tuh deal with him right here an' now! Gimme that shootin' iron, Roy Rogers!"

Roy tried to speak, but Gimlet didn't pause.

"Give it tuh me!" he bellowed, reaching for Roy's holster.

Roy caught Gimlet's skinny wrist. "If anyone has cause to shoot Pritchard," he said, "I'm the one. Now take it easy for a minute."

166

"*You!*" howled Gimlet. "What right've *you* got tuh shoot him? You ain't layin' flat on yer back, all stove in an' busted up by what he done!"

"Who *is?*" demanded Roy quickly.

"Dick Collins, that's who!"

Roy glanced toward the tarpaulin lean-to. He saw Dick's form, motionless, on the blanket.

"What happened?" he demanded.

"You ask what happened?" roared Gimlet. "Come over here. Come over to the derrick an' I'll show yuh what happened. I'll show yuh what that rat-faced, weasel-minded, triple-twisted coyote done! He tried to murder my pard!"

During this blast Gimlet had stalked ahead of Roy to the base of the derrick. Roy saw the heavy bailer lying where it had crashed through the plank flooring. Gimlet grabbed the rope, close to the windlass.

"Lookit this," he bellowed. "Pritchard come here this mornin', posin' as a friend. He an' Dick was a-standin' right here where you're standin.' The bailer fell an' clipped Dick. It would o' been sure death if it'd hit him square. That dirty low-livin' murderer claimed that the rope had busted an' at the time I swallered his lie! The truth is, the rope was cut!" With a hand that shook with the intensity of his anger, Gimlet held the rope so Roy could see the end. "You c'n see fer yerself, Roy! Anyone can see that rope didn't bust from bein' old an' rotted. It was cut clean with a sharp knife. I ain't got no doubt but what we'll find the knife that done it in that rat's pocket."

Roy brushed past Gimlet and ducked into the shelter where Dick lay with eyes closed, his shoulder and upper arm a mass of tight bandages. Roy felt for the pulse and found it strong and steady.

"Who did the bandaging?" he asked.

"The sawbones was here. Doc Martin. He wanted tuh take Dick into town but he refused tuh be took. He insisted on stayin' here, at least until you got back, so's he could keep an eye on the work. The poor kid don't realize that the work on this yere job is finished as of right now. We're through an' we're licked!"

"What did the doctor say?"

"Dick's got a couple of bad gashes an' his collar bone is busted. He's lucky to be alive. The Doc gave him somethin' tuh make him sleep quiet fer a time."

"How did the doctor know about the injury?"

"The polecat that done it told him. I suppose Pritchard figgered that we wouldn't suspect him of cuttin' the rope if he went intuh town an' sent the sawbones here."

Roy's face was grim, his lips drawn into a thin line, as he rose from Dick's side and approached Snag Pritchard.

"What," he demanded, "have you got to say about this?"

"I ain't talkin'," replied Snag.

"Lemme at him," pleaded Gimlet. "Just lemme have five minutes with the long-toothed crook. I'll loosen his tongue."

"No," said Roy, "you won't. He won't talk and I don't think anything you can do will make him."

"He's tuh blame fer everythin' that's happened," Gimlet said. "We might've had a slim chance of bringin' in the oil, if he hadn't come here, but now the bailer's down, an' the rope is busted, an' Dick is busted up, an'—"

"Just a minute," broke in Roy. "You can splice the rope. You've done it before. You can tie the bailer back where it belongs, The broken planks in the derrick won't matter."

"D'you mean tuh say we're tuh go on with the job?"

"Are you going to quit while there's still time to bring in that oil?" demanded Roy.

"But we—"

"Are you going to let Tom down? Are you going to quit because Dick can't work with you?"

Gimlet stared at the speaker in disbelief. "Y-You mean to say," he gasped, "that I should go on all alone?"

"Steve Logan told me you'd *never* quit!"

"Steve Logan!"

"Yes. I've been over to Osage. I met Steve and he told me a lot about you, Gimlet."

"Thar's the finest, squarest man I ever knowed," said Gimlet. "They don't come no finer than Steve Logan!"

"He said practically the same things about you, Gimlet."

"He—he did? Steve said that about me?"

"He was mighty complimentary about you. He said you knew oil land when you saw it. He said you'd get oil from this ground, if you went after it!"

Gimlet's face was a study. He looked at Roy, then at Dick's sleeping form. Then he looked appraisingly at the bailer, punched half through the planks. "I suppose," he finally said, "we could fix that thing up an' go ahead with the job."

"Does the engine work?"

"It does an' it don't. It takes a lot o' coaxin' tuh keep 'er runnin'. But, by Juniper, we c'n do the best we can! They's one thing that's dead certain. That well ain't gushin' no oil as it stands now, an' we ain't a-goin' tuh git no oil if we stand around doin' nothin'!" Gimlet looked at Snag Pritchard. "What about him?" he demanded.

"We're going to keep him here for a few days."

"Whar'd you find the polecat?"

Roy told about the ambush on the trail. "I don't

know why he tried to shoot me," he said. "Maybe
he thinks I learned too much while I was in Osage."

"What *did* yuh learn?"

Roy's reply was enigmatic. "I learned more on the
way back from there than I learned in Osage," he
said.

Gimlet frowned at this and said, "Huh?"

"The fact that Pritchard was lying in wait for me
told me a lot more than anything I heard in Osage.
Now let's get to work. We've got a lot to do."

Roy unwound the lariat which had, until now,
held Snag Pritchard helpless. In its place the cowboy tied short lengths of cord around the killer's
wrists and ankles. In the meantime, Gimlet went to
work on the cable. He unraveled the rope where it
had been cut, then began splicing. His hands were
old and gnarled, and some of his fingers were
slightly crooked from broken bones which had
healed imperfectly, but he did a workmanlike job
of splicing. It was a job even Roy, perfectionist
though he was in many things, thought excellent.

Roy climbed to the top of the derrick and ran the
repaired rope through the pulley. It took the com-
bined strength of the two men to get the heavy
bailer tied on. When this had been done, Gimlet
went to work with the drill.

At sunset Dick Collins opened his eyes and looked
around. Roy, who had been watching, was at his

side in an instant.

"Are—are we licked?" asked Dick in a low, weak voice.

Roy shook his head. "Not yet," he grinned. "Gimlet's hard at it with the drill."

Dick sighed heavily. "The—the doctor wanted to move me to town," he said. "I—I want to stay here."

"I understand."

"Don't let 'em move me, Roy. I—I want to stick with the job as long as it goes on."

"We'll make you as comfortable as we can," Roy told him. "The weather looks clear for another twenty-four hours. If the signs point to a storm, we'll have to get you to a better shelter, but we won't worry about that until it's necessary."

Dick smiled feebly and said, "I knew you'd understand . . ." He saw Snag Pritchard, then looked questioningly at Roy.

Roy told the story of Snag's capture as briefly as possible.

"Maybe you didn't know it," he finished, "but he tried to kill you, too."

"Snag did?"

"He cut the cable on the bailer."

Dick showed his surprise. "But why?" he asked.

Roy shook his head. "I don't know. I've tried to question him, but he won't talk."

"What're you going to do with him?"

"For the time being, we'll hold him right here in camp."

"But why? Why not turn him over to the law?"

"In the first place, Dick, there isn't much we can prove against him. We can't prove he cut the rope, and I can't prove that he was going to drill me on the trail."

"That's so," Dick agreed.

"So we'll hold him here, at least until tomorrow."

For some time Rogers had been considering a plan of action. He had first thought of the plan in the early afternoon, soon after Snag's capture. At that time it had seemed too outlandish and impossible to be given serious consideration. But as the day progressed the idea recurred, and each time he thought of it, it seemed a little less impossible. It might succeed because it *was* so fantastic. By the time Dick wakened, Roy had decided to give it a try.

To Dick he said, "I'm going to ride into Gopher Creek tonight, Dick. I expect to return tomorrow, but, if I don't, don't worry! Tell Gimlet to keep right on with his job. I *will* be back as soon as possible!"

"What are you going to do, Roy?"

"The less you and Gimlet know about it, the better. I'm going to make a move based on a hunch I had after Snag tried to dry-gulch me. It may work, and it may not. We'll find out."

"I guess," muttered Dick, "anything you do will be all right."

"There's one thing you've got to do," said Roy. Dick nodded.

Roy's voice grew softer and more serious than Dick had heard it. "No matter what happens, Dick, *no matter what happens,* remember I'm on your side!"

CHAPTER NINETEEN

After the evening meal, before darkness set in, Roy sat on the ground facing Snag Pritchard.

"There's no use tryin' tuh make me talk," the killer warned. "I ain't goin' to."

"Why not?" asked Roy.

Snag's mouth twisted in a sneer. "D'ya think," he said, "I'm a fool? You got nothin' on me an' you know it, Rogers. Take me to the sheriff an' what'll yuh say? Yuh'll say I cut the rope an' dropped the bailer on Dick's head."

"Possibly," said Roy. "It would be true, wouldn't it?"

"True or not, how'd yuh prove it? Did anyone see me cut the rope? No, they didn't! Can you show where the rope was cut?" Snag laughed. "Yuh can't even do that! It's been spliced so there's nothin' to show whether it broke or got cut. You got nothin' against me, Rogers."

"There's a little matter of waiting in ambush for me."

Snag laughed harshly. "Prove it!" he challenged. "I went tuh town after Dick got hurt, an' sent the doctor tuh help him. Then, feelin' sorry fer him, I

175

went out tuh try an' get a fat grouse so's Gimlet could make my pal a nice stew or maybe some broth. What happened? I'm just takin' aim at a bird when you come jumpin' on me, drag me here an' hold me prisoner!"

"You've worked out a pretty convincing story, haven't you, Pritchard?"

"I'll lay two tuh one it'll stand up! Even if a jury don't believe all of it, they can't shoot holes in it! I got a real case against you, Rogers! As soon as I get away from here, I'm goin' to put you intuh so much legal trouble you'll wish you'd never seen Gopher Creek! If you think you c'n hogtie an' hold a man like you're holdin' me, you'd better think again."

"Just a minute, Snag. Forget the story you're going to tell the law. By the time you get there, the man who hired you to kill people will have told all about your part in the murders. He'll turn State's evidence and let you face the music."

For a moment Snag looked worried, but he recovered quickly and laughed. "Too thin, Rogers. I suppose you figgered me tuh rise to that bait an' tell my story first, eh?"

"Frankly, Pritchard, I don't give a hang whether you talk or not. As soon as I see Dick settled for the night, I'm going into town to have a showdown with your boss. If you want to help your case by telling what you know, this is the time to do it."

"You," snarled Snag, "can go to blazes!"

Roy nodded and rose to his feet. "I'll see you soon," he said.

Snag Pritchard watched the compact figure of the cowboy enter the lean-to to join Dick and Gimlet. Then, as he grunted and squirmed to find a more comfortable position, he saw something gleam in the grass where Roy had been sitting. He glanced quickly back to the lean-to. No one was paying any attention to him. He moved, almost imperceptibly, toward the gleaming object. He moved again, and glanced once more toward his captor. Inching along the ground, bit by bit, he finally came within reach of the knife which had, in some unaccountable manner, slipped from the scabbard on Roy's belt. His hand closed around the leather-bound handle. Then began a period of tense waiting. If only Roy would ride away from there without missing his knife! The minutes dragged heavily. Darkness had never been so long in gathering. Snag didn't dare try to cut the rope. Any effort along that line might attract the attention of one of the three men in the lean-to. He waited as patiently as possible.

At last, Roy made preparations for departure. Snag watched every move with hawklike intensity. He saw Roy and Gimlet make Dick comfortable. A moment later Roy left the shelter, and without looking back, headed for the corral.

Snag breathed a great sigh of relief when he saw the cowboy ride away toward Gopher Creek. After that it was but a matter of seconds. The knife quickly cut the ropes. Snag was free to stand. He kept one eye on the lean-to as he hurried, crouching low, toward the corral. He didn't stop to saddle his horse, but leaped astride the beast's bare back and heeled the animal cruelly.

Gimlet let out a wild yell when he saw what was happening. Snag Pritchard's scornful laugh rang out above the clatter of his horse's hoofs.

After leaving camp, Roy rode at a fast gait for the first few miles. Then he let Trigger fall into his favorite lope for most of the remaining distance. Instead of going directly into town, Roy left the trail for the bed of the creek which gave the community its name. Here he reined up and dismounted.

The bed of the creek was wide and deep enough to accommodate tons of water during spring floods. For the remainder of the year, there was a level space of dry land, several yards wide, on each side of the stream. Roy found that he could wait here, protected by the steep bank from the view of anyone who passed.

"Snag Pritchard showed us how to make use of a place like this," he muttered to Trigger. He tossed the reins over Trigger's head and let them fall to the ground. This was a sign the horse understood. He wouldn't move from the place as long as the reins touched the ground.

"You may have a long wait," Roy whispered to his horse. "Don't get impatient, old boy. I'll be back as soon as I can make it."

He moved to the edge of the bank and settled himself in a comfortable position. He hadn't long to wait. In a few minutes he thought he heard the distant clump of hoofs. A moment later he was sure of it. A horseman was coming over the same trail he had just used.

Roy could have reached out and touched Snag Pritchard's horse, it passed so close to him. He allowed a few seconds for the killer to gain a little distance, then scrambled from his resting place and followed on foot.

Practically all the buildings in the town were on the one main street. This thoroughfare ran parallel to, and south of, the creek. This meant that buildings on the north side of the street had back doors facing the creek, itself. Snag guided his horse through the darkness, along the rear of the row of buildings. He halted at the rear of one of the larger structures.

Running softly and keeping in the darkest shadows, Roy had closed in on Snag by the time he had dismounted and tied his horse.

Snag heard steps and turned as Roy came up. Before he could utter an exclamation of surprise, the killer felt the hard barrel of a gun jabbing his side.

"Keep quiet!" ordered Roy.

Snag gasped a whispered, "You!"

"You'll find out, sooner or later, that there are a lot of ways to make you tell things, Pritchard. Now I'll take back my knife."

"You left it for me to find! You done it on purpose!" hissed Snag.

"Sure," grinned Roy as he jerked the knife from the killer's belt and put it back in the sheath where it belonged. "I let you know I was going to visit your boss. I thought if you had the chance to get ahead of me, you'd lead me to him."

"I—" began Snag Pritchard.

"I wasn't sure whether you'd come to Geesel or head for John Clayton over in Osage."

"Wha . . . what're you goin' to do now?"

"First of all, I'm going to tie and gag you. What I do after that is none of your business." As he spoke, Roy drew slender but exceptionally strong cords from his pocket. He made a few deft passes and captured Snag's hands. "Sit down," he ordered. "If you feel like yelling, just remember what you got a few hours ago. If you don't want more of the same, keep quiet."

Snag sat on the ground.

Roy holstered his gun and tied the killer's feet. Last of all, he gagged Snag Pritchard, using the unprotesting prisoner's own handkerchief.

"I guess that'll hold you for the next half hour," Roy said when his job was finished. "I'll be back for you after I've had a meeting with your boss."

A woodshed's sloping roof leaned against the rear of the store. At the corner stood the rain barrel, and a couple of loose boards lay on the ground to make a dry approach to the water-barrel in wet weather.

Moving quickly and silently, Roy took one of the slabs of wood and laid it across the top of the rain-barrel. This gave him a platform from which his strong fingers could grasp the edge of the wood-shed's roof. He drew himself up, then cautiously, on hands and knees, went toward a window on the second floor.

Back on the ground Snag Pritchard lay still, to give Roy Rogers time to get beyond hearing distance. The killer thought he'd then have little difficulty in tearing apart the slender cords which held him.

CHAPTER TWENTY

ROY'S BIG BLUFF

Though Roy Rogers had been in Abe Geesel's office only once, he had a mental picture of the second floor of the building. He remembered the hall that ran from the front, where the stairs came up, to the window at the rear. He was outside that window now, on the sloping roof.

The window, fortunately, was unlocked. Roy opened it slowly, very slowly, so there would be no rasp or squeak to betray his presence. He reached in and carefully moved the shade to one side. The hall was dark, save for the glow from the street that came up the stairs.

Soundlessly, Roy climbed inside and waited to see if his entry had been noticed. It was important that he find Abe Geesel alone in his room. If there were someone with the moneylender, Roy planned to wait until the caller left. He moved down the hall until he reached Abe Geesel's door, where a ribbon of yellow light signified that Geesel was at home. Roy pressed his ear to the panel and listened. There was no sound.

Satisfied that his man was alone, the cowboy tapped lightly on the door. He heard the bolt moved back and the door opened a narrow crack. Roy shoved hard. The door swung wide, accompanied by an exclamation of surprise.

"What's the idea?" barked Abe Geesel.

Roy stepped into the room and closed the door behind him.

"I want to see you, Geesel," he explained.

Abe Geesel lived in mortal dread of being robbed. He also feared personal injury. He saw the possibility of both these catastrophic things when Roy Rogers came into the room. Stark terror was stamped on his face. He was wild-eyed and his voice trembled.

"Wha-wha-what d-do you w-want?" he stammered.

"Remember me?"

Geesel could only nod.

"I was here with Dick Collins."

"I—I r-remember."

"You seem surprised to see me alive, Geesel. Snag Pritchard isn't a very efficient man, is he?"

"I—I d-don't know wha-what you mean," gasped the lean-faced man.

"I think you do. Now let me tell you something, Geesel. There's a very good chance that I may leave here without hurting you. It depends on you."

"Wha-what d-do you want?"

"In the first place, I want you to stick to the truth.

No lies! Is that clear?"

Abe Geesel nodded.

"Good." Roy sat down in the rickety chair at the end of the desk, leaned back and crossed his knees. "Snag didn't pick a very good place to wait in ambush for me. He was careless," he said in a conversational tone.

Geesel swallowed hard. "D-don't blame me for that," he pleaded. "I—I tried to t-tell Snag. I—"

Roy grinned and said, "That's enough."

Geesel's statement verified all that Roy had suspected. Now he could proceed with no uncertainty about the part Geesel had played in recent events.

"Sit down and stop shaking," said Roy. "Get a grip on yourself. What are you afraid of?"

Geesel sat down in his desk chair and swallowed hard.

"Snag made a mistake," Roy went on, "and he's sorry for it. That account is all squared up. I'm not holding anything Snag tried to do to me, against you."

Relief flooded Geesel's face. "What about Snag?" he asked. "Did you get him?"

Roy nodded and said, "I got him."

Abe glanced at the heavy gun on Roy's thigh.

"He had quite a bit to say," continued Roy, "before I shut him up."

Geesel nodded.

"Sit Down and Stop Shaking," Said Roy

"I came here tonight because of the way Snag has been bungling things, Geesel. I thought there might be a few things you and I could discuss."

"What do you mean?"

"I thought you might have the impression that I was a pretty good friend of Dick Collins."

"Aren't you?" demanded Geesel sharply.

"Don't you realize that I did you more of a favor than I did Collins when I shot away your gun yesterday afternoon?"

"You nearly broke my hand," said Geesel, remembering the crack shooting of the cowboy.

"You were going to kill Dick Collins."

"I—I guess I was. He—he made me so mad I didn't know what I was doing."

"You'd have swung for it."

"Possibly." Geesel's face regained its shrewd expression as his composure returned. "Did you come here to tell me that you saved me from hanging?" he asked.

"Not at all. I came because I thought you'd like to hear the latest report from Collins's camp."

Geesel shook his head. "I'm not interested in what goes on there," he said.

"Don't lie to me!" Roy's voice was so sharp it shook Abe's newly regained composure. "I happen to know the facts, Geesel. Remember that! I know how far you've gone to block that job!"

"I'm not admitting anything."

"I don't care what you admit! Just stick to the truth while I'm here or we won't get far."

Geesel nodded and said, "What are you getting at?"

Up to this point Roy had been on fairly sure ground. His next step was pure bluff. "I'll tell you," he said slowly. "You'll get a one-fourth interest in the well, if Collins is successful. You'll get a lot more, if Collins is *not* successful. It's worth a lot to you, to make sure John Clayton has the chance to buy that land, isn't it?"

Geesel's face was expressionless. For a moment there was nothing said. Roy met the moneylender's cold eyes with a steady gaze. Finally he said, "How much is it worth to you?"

Geesel said, "What is the latest report from Collins's camp?"

Roy could have shouted. His hunch had been right. Now he knew where Clayton stood. He was simply the figurehead. It was Abe Geesel's money which had paid for the option in John Clayton's name. It was Geesel who would own the land if that second option, and not the first, were to be taken up. Geesel's request for information was a tacit admission that he was willing to talk terms.

Geesel, too, was relieved. Now he knew, or thought he knew, why Roy had come to see him.

It was simply a case of a gunman looking for an assignment. This man with the steady eyes and the accurate pistol was simply an improved model of Snag Pritchard.

Roy said, "I told you a little while ago that Pritchard was a bungler. He proved that when he failed to frame Gimlet Lonergan successfully."

Geesel nodded, and Roy inwardly chalked up another proved hunch, as he went on talking.

"He hasn't stopped work on the well. Collins may not be able to work, but Gimlet won't need him. The well's so nearly finished that the old man might bring it in alone."

"You seem to know what you're talking about."

"I make sure of the facts before I talk," replied Roy. "I got pretty well acquainted with young Collins. I even did some work on the job, myself, after I returned from Osage."

"Do you think you could keep Collins from being successful?"

"That," said Roy, "depends."

"A question of money?"

"Several things. In the first place, I've got to be sure you don't send the lawmen to get me after I've pulled your chestnuts from the fire. I don't intend to take any blame for anything that happens."

"Can't you trust me?"

Roy laughed at this absurd statement.

Geesel's face grew red. "Well, all right then," he said unpleasantly. "You needn't laugh in my face."

"I wouldn't trust you, Geesel, any farther than you'd trust me! Does that answer your question?"

"What are your terms?"

"You won't like them, Geesel, but you'd better think carefully before you say no."

"Your terms?"

"Just remember that I'm your last hope of getting all of the oil well instead of twenty-five per cent!"

Geesel nodded.

"It will cost you one thousand dollars."

At this sum Geesel started to protest, but Roy went right on. "There will be no bartering and no discussion. It's a thousand or nothing, and you can take it or leave it. If you're willing to spend that much, I'll give you the rest of the deal."

"The rest," gasped Geesel. "Do you want more?"

"The thousand is the financial side of it."

"What else is there?"

"An agreement for my own protection."

"What kind of an agreement?"

"I don't expect all of the cash until I've delivered the goods. You'll pay two hundred and fifty dollars down and the rest after the first of the month. You see, you don't take as much risk as you thought."

Geesel rather liked this part of the deal. "If you're not successful, I don't pay the balance, is that it?"

"That's it. We'll draw up a simple agreement whereby you agree to pay two-fifty in advance and seven hundred and fifty dollars on the first of the month, if, through my efforts, Dick Collins is blocked in bringing in the oil. You'll notice, Geesel, that I have said, 'Through my efforts.' That means that I've really got to act, to earn my money. I can't just sit back and trust to luck."

"You certainly have thought this thing out in advance."

"Of course, I have."

"But if you think I'll sign any such agreement—"

"You'll sign it, or there's no deal. You're no fool, Geesel. You're a shrewd man. The paper will be a protection for both of us. I can't double-cross you. You can't double-cross me."

Geesel leaned back and thought for a moment. He recalled the receipt with Snag Pritchard's name affixed. The receipt that would prove beyond doubt that Pritchard had killed the three half-breeds. It was a comparable situation. This chap named Rogers wasn't stupid. He was smart.

Roy rose from his seat. "The deal's in your lap, Geesel."

"We should discuss that price a little more. After all, money doesn't grow on trees."

"It'll come out of the ground in your case, Geesel. You have the price."

The money-loving man knew when further discussion was hopeless. He sighed deeply. Then he said,

"All right! I'll accept your terms!"

CHAPTER TWENTY-ONE

When it came to drawing up a document of any sort, there were few who could do a better job than Abe Geesel. Having spent a lifetime taking advantage of every loophole in every kind of contract, he was adept at writing an agreement that had no loopholes. There was just one difficulty about his agreement with Roy Rogers. Roy didn't like it. He rejected the first and second drafts. He suggested changes in the third. Geesel finally worked out a grouping of words that satisfied his stubborn visitor. This he copied on a battered typewriter dragged from somewhere beneath his desk.

"It's simple enough," Roy said when the agreement was finally ready for signing. "You pay me two hundred and fifty dollars in cash when you have seen work on the oil well halted. The balance becomes due and payable on the first of the month, if, because of my efforts in your behalf, Dick Collins is unable to take up his option to buy the Bixby land."

Abe Geesel growled, "It's simple enough. I don't know what was wrong with the first draft."

Roy smiled pleasantly. "It wasn't the way I

wanted it, that's all. This last paragraph is important for your own protection, Geesel. It states that I will turn this agreement over to you, upon receipt of the final payment."

Geesel nodded.

"You see," Roy went on, "I just want to be sure you make the final payment. After that, I'll leave here, and what you do won't matter."

Geesel would never have signed the agreement had there been any other way to secure the services of this efficient young man. Even though his signature wasn't witnessed, it could be identified by a number of people in town. The paper might become a dangerous instrument. He was glad to know he would have it back when he made the final payment of seven hundred and fifty dollars.

If Roy had demanded a thousand dollars cash in advance, Geesel would have balked immovably. A little while ago it had seemed like a sensible idea to pay most of the money *after* the job for which he was paying had been done. Now Geesel had a different point of view. He watched as his visitor carefully folded the agreement and stowed it in an inner compartment in his wallet. His fear began overbalancing his avarice.

"Look here," he said suddenly. "You wanted that agreement so I couldn't cheat you out of your money, didn't you?"

"Partially," said Roy.

"I'll tell you what I'll do. I hate to have a paper like that running around loose."

"Loose?"

"I mean, out of my possession. If something happened to you and that paper were found, I'd be in a bad situation."

"Very bad," replied Roy with a smile. "You'd better make sure nothing happens to me."

"We don't need that document at all," said Geesel. "I'll pay you in full right now."

Roy couldn't believe his ears. It was unheard-of for Geesel to hand out such a sum.

"I'll give you the cash right now and you give me back the paper."

"It's against my rules to take cash I haven't earned," replied Roy.

"It's all right. I'm confident you'll earn it. I can size a man up. I'll trust you."

"But," said Roy, "I won't trust you."

"What do you mean? You'll have your money in advance! How can I double-cross you?"

"Very easily. You could have the law crack down on me as soon as I make a move against the machinery at the camp. I'd have done my job, only to find myself arrested. You'd say I was a crook and the evidence would back you up. You'd further state that I came here and stole a thousand dollars from you at the point of a gun. You'd get your money back, you'd block Collins and Gimlet, and I'd spend a long time in jail."

Geesel gasped at the way Roy so easily outlined what would have been a beautiful situation—from Geesel's point of view.

"That," finished Roy, "is why I don't trust you, Geesel. Now we've got to make a date."

"A—a date?"

"Why, yes," replied Roy easily. "You remember the agreement. You should, you've written it over enough. You're to pay me two hundred and fifty dollars when you've seen work on the oil well halted."

"But I—"

"That means you've got to *see* it!"

"I don't want to be involved in—"

"Geesel, are you backing out on the agreement?"

"Now wait a minute, Rogers. Hold on. I—"

"It's a good thing I have the agreement in writing. You're already trying to back out."

"Nothing of the sort. I'm not backing out. It's simply that I don't need to *see* what you do! I'll take your word. I'll trust you to go ahead and—"

"No," interrupted Roy. "We're going to do just what we agreed. What are you worried about, Geesel? Do you think *I'm* going to let myself get caught? Don't you suppose you'll be safe enough with me?"

"I—I don't know," faltered Geesel, who was beginning to have genuine doubts. "I can't understand you."

"I'll meet you tomorrow afternoon."

"Where?"

"At Collins's camp, of course."

"At—at the c-camp?"

"Your money's invested there. Is there any reason why you shouldn't go out and see how the work is progressing?"

"W-Well, n-no, I—I guess not—"

"Then I'll meet you there at three o'clock."

"I—I'll try to make it."

"You'd better!" said Roy with a note of warning in his voice. He tapped the pocket holding his wallet. "You'd better be there!" he repeated.

He opened the door, then quickly closed it from the outside.

Geesel hurried to the dirty window, but though he watched for the next ten minutes, he didn't see Roy Rogers leave the building. He didn't know the horseman had hurried down the hall to leave by the same way he had entered.

Roy slid down the sloping roof at the rear of the building. He swung himself over the edge, hung for a moment by his hands, then dropped lightly to the ground.

"Is everything all right with you, Snag?" he greeted pleasantly. "Don't try to answer me."

He tested the ropes and the gag and found them as secure as they had been when he'd knotted them in place. "Sorry to keep you waiting. I'm not through yet."

Leaving Pritchard to think things over, Roy hurried along the rear of the row of buildings until he was well away from the general store and Geesel's office. Then he went through a narrow space to the street.

His plans called for a visit with the sheriff. He found Jim Lambert working overtime in his office.

"What are you doing in town?" the sheriff said, as Roy walked through the door. "I thought you'd gone to Osage."

"I've been back from there for some time, Sheriff. In fact, I spent most of the afternoon at the camp."

"I heard about Dick's accident. That sure is tough. The poor chap. He's had things pile up on him."

"Have you found the murderer of the half-breeds?"

Lambert shook his head. "No, and I don't know as I ever will. There's nothing to work with!"

Roy sat down on the edge of the sheriff's desk. "Unless you've objections," he said, "I'd like to help find him."

"You?"

Roy nodded.

"I've no objections, Rogers, but what's on your mind?"

Roy grinned. "It's a long story," he said. "I'll start at the beginning."

For ten minutes Roy talked in a low voice. Jim Lambert nodded frequently, but didn't interrupt. Toward the end of Roy's amazing narrative, the lawman's eyes widened in surprise. His face took on a look of anger and his hands closed into hard fists. Roy unfolded his plans and the sheriff's eyes lost their dark, intense expression and began to twinkle in amusement. When the story was finished, the big man slapped his desk and said, "By thunder, Rogers! I think you've got something!"

"Then you'll let me help?"

"Let *you* help! Why, hang it all, *I'm* the one that'll be helpin', and that suits me! Go ahead, Rogers. I've been sheriff for twenty-two years and I've never heard of anything to equal this!"

CHAPTER TWENTY-TWO

KILLER AT LARGE

Snag Pritchard had remained quiet while Roy Rogers climbed from the water barrel to the roof of the woodshed on his way to see Abe Geesel. The killer had waited a few minutes more to give Roy time to get inside the building. He was tied about the wrists and ankles in such a way that his hands were held close to his feet and his body bent at the waist. It was an awkward position which gave little freedom of movement.

Snag began his fight for freedom with a frenzy born of blinding anger. He pitted his own brute strength against the strength of the slender cord. First he tried to tear the rope apart by tugging. Then he jerked at it and tried to twist it. He threshed on the ground in his struggles; he strained until his clothes were soaked with sweat and breathing was torture. The gag made it impossible to gulp air through his mouth. His nostrils couldn't suck air fast enough to supply the demands of his lungs. His heart throbbed and he could feel the pulse hammering in his throat and temples. Yet he continued to fight. His wrists were cut and bleeding and his hands were numb, but there was no feeling of pain.

The killer's insane lust for revenge made him oblivious to pain. His desperation was like that of the trapped animal that bites off its own foot to gain freedom.

The rope couldn't be broken. It wouldn't stretch. Snag finally had to quit this line of attack from utter exhaustion.

He lay on his right side, gathering strength for a renewed effort. His breathing finally returned to normal, and when Roy returned, the killer was quiet. The cowboy felt the ropes in the darkness and found them tight. He tested the gag and found this as he had left it. Then he went away.

Snag squirmed until he gained a sitting position. This was a little better than lying on the ground, but it was a strain on his back to sit, with his hands held to within a few inches of his feet by a short length of cord. He inched along the ground until he was against the rear wall of the woodshed. This braced his back and relieved the tension on his wrists.

In adjusting himself, his boot clanked against something metallic. He thought nothing of it at first, but a moment later he realized that he might have found a working tool. The water barrel was fed by a downspout which carried rainwater from a gutter along the edge of the roof. A section of this trough had fallen or been blown to the ground during a recent storm.

He felt around with his hands, and soon located the six-foot length of galvanized iron trough. He tested its edge with his fingers, but found it rounded and quite smooth. Squirming with feverish haste, he felt along the length of the metal until he reached one end. Here the tinsmith's shears had left a sharp edge. A cutting edge! Snag made the most of this. Working his hands back and forth, he soon sawed through the length of line between his hands and feet. It parted and he could move more freely.

He maneuvered to a better working position. Kneeling on the ground, he clamped the gutter between his thighs. Then he pressed the rope against the sharp edge and began working his hands and arms slowly back and forth. He was handicapped by darkness, and when his hands slipped he got a jagged cut on one wrist, but this was nothing compared with what awaited him if he didn't escape. He was inspired by the nearness of his freedom and the prospect of revenge.

The rope began to fray. It parted, strand by strand, and at last the killer's hands were free. He tore the gag from his mouth, then began clawing at the knots on his ankles. These were hopelessly tight as a result of his own straining and pulling. He broke his fingernails before he realized it would be impossible to untie the ropes. Then he resorted to the gutter once more and finally his feet were released.

At first he found it difficult to stand. He staggered to the rainbarrel and plunged his hands in deep. He dashed water on his face, then ducked his whole head. He came up dripping, but refreshed.

"Now," he gloated, "to square a few accounts with Roy Rogers!"

He needed a weapon, but almost anything would do. He hurried to the side of the woodshed where the chopping block stood, and felt around on the ground until he found a short length of wood.

"This'll do," he muttered. "I'll have Rogers's gun soon after he gets back here."

Roy Rogers whistled softly as he walked through the faint starlight in the rear of the row of buildings. He was pleased with the way things had worked out. His evening had been wholly satisfactory, and he anticipated surprising developments in the very near future.

As he neared the rear of the general store, he saw Snag Pritchard on the ground, in the same position in which Roy had left him nearly an hour ago.

"I'm sorry to keep you waiting," Roy said as he halted beside Snag. "I'll ungag you now. Then I'll untie your feet so you can ride. We're going to camp by ourselves for the rest of the night."

When he squatted beside Snag Pritchard and reached out to remove the gag, he saw, to his dismay, that the handkerchief on Snag's mouth wasn't tied. He had a fleeting glimpse of the murderer in sudden movement and an instant to realize that Snag was free, before the blow.

Snag struck hard. The length of wood crashed on Roy's head.

Partially stunned, he tried to defend himself, but Snag was on his feet. His arm came up and fell again. This time there was more power behind the blow. Roy had a momentary glimpse of a dazzling array of white and red lights, then he felt himself sinking into a black, bottomless void of complete oblivion.

"This," gloated Snag Pritchard, "is goin' to be good!"

Snag wasn't one to act on his own initiative. He could follow orders with ruthless precision, but his ability to make his own decisions was strictly limited. He stood over the unconscious cowboy, uncertain as to what his next move should be. He half raised the heavy chunk of wood to deliver another blow, then changed his mind. He wanted to kill the young man, but thoughts of Abe Geesel's ire rose in his mind to block him. He decided to consult Abe before making another move.

He disarmed his victim and stuck the cowboy's

gun in his own holster. Then he looked around for something with which to tie the helpless man while he sought instructions from his friend, the money-lender. There was rope in the woodshed. Snag found this and clumsily wound it many times around Roy's arms and body.

"That'll hold him for a few minutes," Snag muttered. "It won't take long tuh see what Geesel wants done with the critter."

CHAPTER TWENTY-THREE

RECOVERY

Roy felt as if he were in the grip of a whirlpool. He had a giddy sensation of spinning like a top. When he opened his eyes, he thought he'd gone blind, but gradually his eyes focused on faint stars overhead. His head throbbed frightfully. The slightest move brought stabbing shots of pain to his temples and the base of his skull.

He remembered talking to Abe Geesel and the sheriff, and as the whirling, spinning sensation subsided, he remembered seeing Snag Pritchard sprawled on the ground. Then he knew what had happened. Snag had, in some unaccountable way, escaped from the cords that held him.

Why, then, was Roy still alive? Surely the killer had had ample opportunity for murder. It was remarkable that the blows with the stick hadn't been fatal. They would have been, Roy thought, had their force not being partially absorbed by his high-crowned Stetson hat.

Roy's mind cleared rapidly. As he gathered his scattered wits, he was stunned by a realization of the importance of getting free. Dick's future and that of Gimlet, the capture of two murderers, the

205

defeat of the scheming moneylender, all depended on him. How long had he been unconscious? Was it a matter of hours or minutes? Why hadn't Snag gagged him? Why, in fact, hadn't the killer struck with the same ruthless permanence that he had applied to the three half-breeds?

One thing only was certain. He had to get free in the shortest possible time. Rolling over on the ground he twisted his head to examine the ropes. He was wrapped in half-inch line from his shoulders to his hips. It was a clumsy job of roping, but temporarily effective. He couldn't move either arms or hands, but, if the rope were cut in just one place, the whole cocoon would slip away.

Roy saw Snag Pritchard's horse, tied where the outlaw had left it, and knew he planned to return, perhaps to finish his job.

How far away was Trigger? Roy had left the palomino in the basin of Gopher Creek to follow Snag on foot. He couldn't remember with any degree of accuracy how far he had come after dismounting. He whistled softly. It was a signal Trigger knew, one to which he would instantly respond, if he heard it. Roy listened and heard no response. He whistled again, a little louder.

Roy heard the steady undercurrent of men's voices from the Silver Dollar and the occasional clump of horses' hoofs. Somewhere in the distance a car started. There were katydids in the near-by grass, but there was no responsive sound from Trigger.

A louder whistle might be the last. If Snag heard it, and knew his captive was conscious, he'd lose no time in getting to the scene. Roy decided to take that chance. He pursed his lips, and a single sharp, piercing note split the night. Roy's heart leaped when his signal was answered. From somewhere in the darkness came a responsive whinny, followed by the clatter of approaching hoofs.

Trigger came up fast.

"Down," ordered Roy. "Down, boy."

Trigger nuzzled his master gently, then felt along the ropes with his velvety nostrils.

"You know what to do, Trigger. Bite 'em!"

Trigger knew exactly what to do. He felt along the ropes until he found a place to grip with his strong teeth. He tugged at this, until he had enough slack to take a firmer grip. Then he started biting.

"You'll have to hurry, Trigger," Roy said softly.

Trigger braced his front legs and pulled on the rope. Roy was lifted off the ground, then lowered. Trigger chewed some more. It took several minutes for the intelligent animal to sever the length of line, but finally it parted and Roy squirmed to his feet. Shifting his shoulders first one way, and then another, he loosened the coils to give his hands freedom. Then he could work faster.

"Be out of this in just a second, Trigger," he said, as coil after coil of the rope fell to his ankles. "Then we'll see where Snag Pritchard went."

Snag Pritchard was in Geesel's office. He told of Roy's capture. "I figure he's got to be rubbed out," he summarized, "but I thought I'd better see you first."

Geesel had recovered from the shock of seeing Snag alive.

"You," he said, "are a bungling fool."

"What d'yuh mean?"

"You told Rogers all about my plans! You let him outwit you at every turn, and—"

"Hold on, Geesel. I didn't tell him a thing."

"Don't lie to me!" snapped the moneylender. "If you didn't tell him, where did he get his information?"

"How do I know?"

"You failed when you tried to frame Gimlet for murder. You failed when you tried to kill Dick Collins. I sent you to get Roy Rogers, and instead of that, you let him capture you."

"But I got away from him."

"Did you search him?"

"No, but I got his gun."

"More incompetence," spat Geesel. "If you'd gone

"Hold on, Geesel. I Didn't Tell Him a Thing."

through his pockets, you'd have found an agreement, signed by me. I hired Rogers!"

"You hired him?" repeated Snag. "For what?"

"To do what you haven't done, you blundering fool! I wasn't exactly happy about having to give him a signed agreement, but it was the only way I could get him to work for me."

"He'll double-cross you and throw us both in jail," howled Snag.

"He made a promise, Pritchard, and unlike you, that man is one who will keep his word."

"How d'yuh know he will?"

"How do I know?" roared the moneylender. "Do you think a man can be in my business all these years without being able to judge a man? He may be willing to hire out for a job like I gave him, but he's no liar. If I didn't know when a man is telling me the truth, I'd have been broke a long time ago."

Geesel sat on the cot and pulled on his shoes. "I'll go and see him," he said. "Perhaps I can persuade him to work for me without that signed agreement."

"But if you let him go, Geesel, what'll he do tuh me?"

"Now that you're out of his hands, it might be a good idea for you to get away from Gopher Creek."

Geesel jerked the door open. "Come on," he said.

As Snag stepped through the door, he felt a tug at his side and heard a sharp command.

"Steady!" said Roy Rogers.

Snag turned quickly, and gasped as he found himself staring at the gun which had been snatched from his own holster.

Geesel, standing near, wore an expression of disdain.

"So," he sneered, "you had him captured!"

Roy grinned at the moneylender.

"I don't know," he said, "how much you've already paid this man for what he did, but whatever it was, you overpaid him."

To Snag he said, "Where did you learn to tie knots?"

"H-How—how did you g-get away?" gasped Pritchard, his hands lifted to his shoulders.

"Were you going somewhere, Geesel?" inquired Roy.

"I was going to see if this rat-faced idiot told me the truth."

"Snag and I are on our way to camp," replied Roy. "We're going to camp alone tonight. I'll take him with me when I go to Collins's camp tomorrow afternoon."

"Why are you taking him there?"

"To make sure he doesn't turn tattler between now and then."

Geesel said, "You let me think you'd killed him."

"I'm not responsible for what you think, Geesel."

"You said you'd got him."

"I have."

Roy prodded the killer with his gun. "Turn around," he said, "and start walking!"

To Geesel he said, "I'll see you tomorrow. You'd better keep your date."

"It isn't necessary for me to be there," replied Geesel in a last appeal.

"You'll be there," replied Roy, "or I'll come and get you!"

CHAPTER TWENTY-FOUR

GIMLET WORKS ALONE

Gimlet wakened, bathed in perspiration. He had been dreaming about Dick's accident, and the dream had been much more vivid than reality. He had seen Snag's evil face, twisted by a gloating grin that exposed the yellow fangs. He saw the killer's hand in a sort of close-up as it knifed through the cable. He saw the bailer falling. It seemed to fall slowly, ever so slowly, but Gimlet was frozen to a spot and could neither move nor shout a warning. Then he saw Dick fall, but in the dream Dick didn't partially avoid the blow. He was just about to be crushed, when Gimlet wakened.

The old man was badly shaken by his dream. He sat bolt upright beneath the shelter and told himself that it had been a dream, but he had to light a candle and examine his young friend before he could lie down again.

Then he lay awake for a long time, haunted by more worries than he could count. He thought of Roy Rogers pursued by Snag Pritchard, the killer creeping up on the cowboy under cover of darkness and stabbing with a silent knife. At last he fell into a fitful sleep, to be tortured by more dreams of violence. He wakened frequently, each time surprised to find that dawn was hours away. This night, it seemed, time stood still.

The old man finally threw back the blanket and got up, since there was no use in trying to sleep. He pulled on his boots and lighted his pipe. He sucked the briar until it burned out and grew cold. Then he walked to the corral and back. He stretched out on the ground and closed his eyes, but now all desire to sleep was gone. He was wide awake and ready to start another day.

In darkness he prepared to cook breakfast, going slowly about each detail of this task, taking as long as possible in order to make the time pass. He built up the fire under the coffee pot. When this had boiled, he drank a cup before proceeding.

Gimlet had never been so glad to see daylight, but his happiness was short lived, because the first faint, gray light revealed a new catastrophe.

On the platform near the engine which operated the drilling machinery, there stood a large pool of water.

The engine was old and had caused a lot of trouble, but Gimlet had managed to keep it running after a fashion. Now he saw with dismay that the boiler had sprung a leak.

Gimlet was too staggered to comment. With a sigh of resignation, he inspected the boiler. First he went over all the connections and found them dry. Then he went over every inch of the water tank, starting at the top and working down. Halfway to the bottom he found a spot brown and corroded with rust.

"That's likely the place," he told himself.

A pail of water stood near by. Gimlet tossed the dipper to one side and emptied the water into the tank. A tiny stream shot out at the rusted place.

The old fellow found a bit of wood, sharpened it to a long point and inserted this into the hole, hammering it tight with a heavy wrench. The hole was plugged, but Gimlet's job had just begun. Water had to be carried from the near-by spring. It took more trips than the old man could count to fill the big tank from the small pail.

"Trouble is," complained Gimlet, "this is just the start. When a tank like that starts goin' in one place, it goes in others. There's likely to be a dozen leaks before the day is over."

The sun was well above the horizon and Dick was awake when Gimlet finally had the fire in the boiler lighted.

Gimlet sat down to rest beside the shelter, and wiped sweat from his face with his faded, tattered shirtsleeve.

"Even with the engine goin', there ain't much use in goin' on," he muttered. "Roy's gone an' I can't do much alone."

Dick said, "I know it, Gimlet. Let's call it all off."

Gimlet's face was drawn and haggard as he looked at Dick.

"I dunno, son," he said, "what tuh say tuh that. I hate like sin tuh give up."

"There might be some sense in going on," replied Dick, "if I could help, but I can't do a thing."

"I know yuh can't."

"You haven't heard from Roy Rogers?"

Gimlet shook his head. "Not a word."

Dick lay quietly for some time.

"Roy spoke of Steve Logan," he said.

"He's a good friend o' mine," replied the old man. "They don't come no better than Steve."

"Wouldn't he give you a job at his place, Gimlet?"

Gimlet looked at Dick. "I reckon he would," he said. "He's allus been mighty fine about givin' a hand tuh an old, stove-in critter that's past his prime. Yup, I reckon Steve Logan would give me a job, if I went askin' for it."

"Why don't you do that, Gimlet?"

"What about you?"

"Just get me into Gopher Creek. I'll be able to get around in a day or so. I'll find something to do."

Gimlet kicked at the ground. "I dunno," he said, "what tuh do. Tom would hate to see us quit."

"If there were any chance at all of getting the oil,

I'd think it worth while to try to hang on, Gimlet, but there isn't. You can't do everything without help, and I'm not worth a tin dime."

"We've got explosive enough tuh fire one blast in the hole," suggested Gimlet. "I suppose I might drill 'er down as far as I can, then give 'er one torpedo an' see what happens."

"What's the drill situation?"

"We still got our last drill. I c'n sharpen 'er up a little an' do my best."

"I think I can sit up, Gimlet. I *might* be able to help."

"You ain't a-goin' tuh, Dick. You know what the Doc said. You gotta take it easy an' stay down." The old man's face broke into a slow grin. "You'd try sittin' though, wouldn't yuh?"

Dick nodded.

"Meanin' that you'd try dang near anything, sooner than see us quit."

"You can't do it alone."

"By thunder," resolved Gimlet, "I c'n try. An' that's just what I'm a-goin' tuh do!"

Gimlet prepared a substantial breakfast for himself and Dick, then sat at his young friend's side and helped him eat. By the time the meal was finished, there was steam pressure in the boiler. Then Gimlet went to work.

He drilled carefully to make that last drill last. He

worked steadily, chattering like a magpie to Dick. After hours of drilling he lowered the bailer and cleaned out the hole. Then he drilled some more. At noon he paused to fix a simple meal which he ate with Dick, showing more enthusiasm than he felt.

"At least, we're makin' headway," he said. "I'll keep goin' a few days without help, an' by then you'll be able to get around. We ain't licked yet, Dick. Not by a jugful."

Before resuming work after the noonday meal, Gimlet went to the small shed and inspected the explosive supply. There was, he estimated, enough to fire one good charge at the bottom of the hole. He decided to continue drilling as long as the last drill held up. Then he'd fire a torpedo-charge and trust to luck and the guardian angels of sincere men.

He checked the steam pressure of the boiler before he resumed the tedious job of drilling. From time to time he glanced across the plain toward Gopher Creek. Still no sign of Roy Rogers. He wished he knew what had happened to the young cowboy.

It was mid-afternoon when he paused in the drilling to lower the bailer. He stood at the controls and the windlass began turning slowly. The rope unwound as the heavy bailer went deeper and deeper into the ground. It touched the bottom of the shaft. Gimlet threw the machinery into neutral. Then he heard the hoofbeats.

Toward Gopher Creek he saw two horsemen. He squinted into the distance until he was sure that one of those horses was a palomino. The next instant he recognized the easy grace with which Roy Rogers rode. His yell might have been heard all the way to Gopher Creek.

"It's Roy!" the old man shouted.

Dick turned on the ground.

"D'ya hear that, Dick? D'ya hear what I say? Roy Rogers is comin' back, a-ridin' lickety-cut."

Gimlet was hopping up and down with joy. His spirits had leaped from low ebb to the peaks at the mere sight of the oncoming cowboy.

"He's got Snag Pritchard, too. He's captured that ornery polecat again. He's a-bringin' him back here so's I can deal with him like I want. Now we'll make things hum! Now, by Juniper, we'll make the dirt fly!"

Just then, in the middle of this enthusiastic outburst, there came a *pop!* and the hissing of steam. Gimlet leaped instinctively. The boiler had sprung a new leak. A great cloud of steam shot from a large hole near the top of the big tank.

Gimlet stared. The full force of this new setback hit him in one blow. This time the boiler couldn't be repaired. The hole was too large. Worst of all, the bailer was at the bottom of the shaft. The hole couldn't be torpedoed until the bailer was removed, and the bailer couldn't be removed without steam-power to run the windlass. Gimlet's soaring spirits fell as fast as the steam pressure. This must be the end.

CHAPTER TWENTY-FIVE

"DON'T BE SURPRISED"

The ruined boiler dampened Gimlet's enthusiasm, but he was none the less glad to see Roy Rogers rein up near the derrick and dismount. He untied one end of his lasso, the end around the saddlehorn. Gimlet saw that the other end was tied around Snag Pritchard's wrists.

"Here we are, Pritchard," Roy said as he went to the side of the killer's unsaddled horse. "I'll help you down."

"I c'n get down without no help," growled the sour-faced crook. He threw his right leg over, turned sideways, and slid clumsily to the ground.

"How's Dick?" asked Roy.

"He's gettin' along as good as you c'd expect," replied Gimlet, "but look what's happened to our machinery!"

Roy looked at the boiler from which thin wisps of steam still issued. "What happened?"

"She's started bustin' out in leaks. I fixed one of 'em, but that last one is too big. There ain't no use fixin' it, anyhow. There'll be more as soon as the pressure is built up." The old man sighed heavily. "We're licked, Roy."

"Not yet," replied the cowboy. "Give me a hand, we've a lot of things to do."

"They's just one thing tuh do," replied Gimlet, glowering at Snag Pritchard. "I'm dang glad yuh brought that polecat back here so's I can do it."

"Do what?"

"Finish him."

"We'll finish him later," said Roy.

"Why not now? Just lemme borrow yore gun fer a minute. I'll deal with the rat."

"Not now, Gimlet. There are other things to do. We'll deal with Snag before sunset."

"Is that a promise?"

Roy nodded. "How is the supply of explosive?" he asked.

"I've got just about enough tuh fire one charge, but I can't use it, Roy. The bailer is down at the bottom of the hole, an' we can't get 'er out without machinery."

"Will you get that explosive for me?"

Gimlet looked bewildered. "But I was just sayin' that we can't fire a torpedo in the well."

"Who said anything about firing a torpedo?"

"Then why d'you want the explosive?"

Roy looked at Snag Pritchard, then turned back to Gimlet and winked.

Gimlet's eye went wide and a grin broke out on his wrinkled face. "Are you goin' to blow the critter to smithereens?" he asked hopefully.

"Not exactly. But we're going to use the dynamite to put an end to his career."

"Hain't that the same as what I said?"

"No," grinned Roy. "There's a difference."

"I'll go git the stuff." Gimlet trotted toward the shed where the blasting materials were stored.

Roy invited Snag Pritchard to sit on the ground and make himself comfortable, then he ducked into the shelter and sat beside Dick Collins.

"How do you feel, Dick?" he asked.

Dick Collins shook his head. "I'd rather lose this arm than see poor old Gimlet licked," he said.

"I can understand how you feel."

"The old fellow has been counting the days until the time he'd have an oil well of his own. This was his one big chance."

Roy nodded.

Dick went on, "You don't know him as well as I do, Roy. He does a lot of talking, but he isn't nearly as bloodthirsty as he makes people think. His heart's as big as all outdoors. You should have seen him all morning, working alone on that job. He didn't let up for a minute."

Roy said, "Dick, there's something I've got to ask you."

Dick looked questioningly at the cowboy.

"I want to know if you think there's a chance to

bring in oil before the deadline."

"You want an honest opinion?"

Roy said, "Of course."

Dick shook his head slowly as he lay on the blanket. "Roy, there wasn't a chance in the world of getting the oil when the engine was operating. We only had one drill, and when that broke, we were through. It couldn't have lasted long, not even with Gimlet handling it."

"That's about the way I sized up the situation."

"Now," continued Dick, "with the boiler gone— well, there wasn't any chance before, and there's even less now."

"Then you won't mind if I try something?"

"You?"

Roy grinned and nodded.

"What d'you want to try?"

"It's probably the most loco stunt you ever heard of, Dick, but if it works, nothing else matters. Isn't that right?"

"Sure, but I—"

"It would take an hour for me to go into details. I had the idea yesterday afternoon. I thought it over, and the more I thought about it, the better I liked it. That's why I left my knife for Snag Pritchard to find."

"You left your knife?"

"Yeah. I wanted him to think he was escaping."

"You intended him to ride away last night?" asked Dick in surprise.

"Sure thing. I let him get past me when I was near Gopher Creek. I wanted to see where he'd go. He went to see Abe Geesel."

"He did, eh?" responded Dick. He looked toward the glum-faced murderer sitting on the ground a few yards away. "So Geesel and he were working together!"

"You must've suspected that, Dick."

Dick nodded slowly. "I hated to think about it, but I guess I had a feeling that Geesel was behind a lot of our trouble."

"I had a long talk with Abe Geesel."

"Last night?"

Roy said, "Yes. He promised to ride out here this afternoon. He should be coming along any minute."

"Geesel? Coming here?"

"Uh-hum," said Roy casually. "There'll be a lot going on in a little while, Dick. Don't be surprised at *anything!*"

Dick laughed softly. "You sure have my curiosity worked up."

"Just remember what I said, Dick. Don't be surprised at *anything!*"

"O.K.," agreed Dick Collins.

Gimlet came up at a trot, carrying a small, cloth sack. "Here's the works," he called.

Roy opened the sack and glanced at a few sticks of dynamite. Then he tossed the sack to the ground.

"The caps an' fuse are in there with the explosive," explained Gimlet.

"All right," said Roy. "Now we've got to break camp."

"Break camp?" repeated Gimlet in surprise. "Why?"

"When that stuff lets go, there might be pieces of iron flying around here. We don't want Dick to stop any of them." As he spoke, Roy pulled the pegs that held the ground edge of the lean-to. He folded the tarpaulin over, then untied the edge fastened to the base of the derrick. "We won't need this any more," he said.

Gimlet watched.

"Do you suppose we can carry Dick over near the corral?" asked Roy.

"I'll take his feet," said Gimlet.

In a few minutes food supplies, blankets, and other things which had been near the lean-to were carried to the new campsite near the high corral.

"If the sun gets too hot," Roy told Dick, "we'll put up the shelter."

"It won't," said Dick. "Not today."

Roy moved Snag to the corral, a few yards from where Dick lay. He made sure the killer couldn't escape, then laid out a few short lengths of rope near the blankets spread beneath the injured man.

Gimlet watched questioningly. "If you'd only tell a curious old galoot what this is all about," he finally said.

Roy said, "Now we'll fuse the dynamite."

He dumped the contents of the bag to the ground. Gathering all the sticks of explosive together, he tied them into a bundle. With a pencil he poked a hole into the waxy dynamite and inserted a cap to which was attached a short length of fuse.

"I guess that will do," he said when he had finished."

Gimlet looked hopeful. "Are yuh goin' tuh put that under Snag Pritchard before yuh light 'er up?" he asked.

"Uh-uh." replied Roy.

"When *are* we goin' to rid the world of that critter?"

Roy looked at his watch and said, "Pretty soon. It won't be long now."

Gimlet saw a horseman in the distance. Roy glanced up at the faint sound of hoofbeats. "Right on time," he commented.

"Who is it?" demanded Gimlet.

"Abe Geesel."

"Why is *he* comin' here?"

Roy rose to his feet. "You'll soon know the answer to everything, Gimlet," he said. "Now stick out your hands. I'm going to tie you up."

Gimlet let out a yell. "Like fun you are! What sort o' trick is this?"

"Sorry, Gimlet, but that's the way it's got to be. Don't make me use force."

Gimlet's good eye blazed with uncomprehending fury.

"Of all the triple-distilled, two-time double-crosses," he raged, "this takes first prize!"

Roy captured the old man's wildly waving arms and tossed a loop about them. A few deft moves and Gimlet was helplessly tied, but by no means silenced. While he ranted and stormed at the sudden change in Roy, the cowboy turned to Dick and said, "I'll have to toss a loop on you, too, Dick."

Dick couldn't understand this move, but he remembered what Roy had said: "Don't be surprised at anything that happens."

CHAPTER TWENTY-SIX

Gimlet's battered, weather-beaten face was purple with rage at what he considered the rankest double-cross he'd ever seen. Nothing Dick or Roy could say would quiet the old man. He stormed and fumed, he raved and ranted, and all the while he fought against the rope that held him. Sheer exhaustion quieted him. Then Dick had a chance to speak.

"You crazy old galoot," he broke in before Gimlet started on another tirade, "take it easy and see what's back of all this. Roy's got some reason for tying us up."

"Tyin' *you*," gasped Gimlet with what little breath he had left. "Tyin' *you*, when you're already so busted up that you can't stand on yer feet!"

"If you'd calm down long enough to look at the rope around me, you'd see that it's as loose as a size-sixteen collar would be on your scrawny neck."

"Huh?" said Gimlet in surprise. "It is?"

"Of course it is."

Abe Geesel had arrived and Roy stood beside the moneylender's horse while he dismounted.

"Now shut up," said Dick to Gimlet, "so you can

listen to what goes on."

"I'll try," muttered Gimlet, "but it ain't goin' tuh be easy."

"I see you've got them tied up," said Abe Geesel.

"That's right."

Geesel was nervous. He dry-washed his hands and shifted his weight from one foot to the other and back again. "I don't see why you insisted that I come here," he said. "You could have carried out your instructions without me."

"We discussed that last night," replied Roy. "I want to be sure you're just as deeply involved as I am. In that way, you see, Geesel, I know you won't try to throw all the blame on me."

Geesel eyed Dick and Gimlet. "They'll have plenty to say to the sheriff," he complained.

"What of it? You're a respected man in Gopher Creek. It will be your word against theirs. The word of a rich, substantial citizen against a couple of men who have reason to be angry at you. Furthermore, you'll have Snag Pritchard to back you up in anything you say."

"That's so," agreed Geesel.

At this point Snag broke in on the dialogue.

"See here," he snarled, "I've been a prisoner long enough, Geesel. Make Rogers untie me. If I'm on your side, why've I got to sit here, tied up like those other two?"

"It's out of my hands," replied Geesel. "This is Rogers's party."

Roy took a folded paper from his pocket. Spreading it flat on the rump of Geesel's horse, he studied it, then said, "Now, Geesel, according to the terms of our agreement, you're to pay me two hundred and fifty dollars when you have seen work on this job permanently halted. You're the one to decide whether the destruction is permanent. Did you bring the money?"

Geesel squirmed uneasily.

From Gimlet there came a howl of rage.

Geesel said, "Is it necessary to let those two know all the details?"

Roy smiled and said, "Why not?"

"If I'd known you brought me here to verify that agreement in front of Collins and Gimlet—"

"I asked you if you brought the cash!"

Geesel nodded.

"All right, then. Stop worrying. You can always hire Snag to commit a few murders, if worse comes to worst."

"What," asked Geesel, "are you going to do?"

"I'll show you."

Roy picked up the fused and capped explosive and carried it to the engine. He opened the door of the firepot and saw a ruddy mass of glowing coals. He tossed the bundle to the fire, then hurried to a safe distance.

A sheet of flame leaped up where the engine had been standing. Metal flew in all directions, and smoke mushroomed upward. The ground shook, and for several seconds there was a rain of twisted metal and broken bits of iron.

Gimlet's shoulders sagged and his head dropped forward on his chest. His Adam's apple moved up and down as he swallowed hard. His voice shook when he spoke. "After all—all our work," he said. "That's the end of it."

"Steady, Gimlet," Dick whispered. "Steady now. Don't be surprised at anything."

Roy turned to Geesel when the rain of metal had stopped. "Are you satisfied?" he demanded.

"I—I guess so," replied the moneylender.

"Work can't proceed without an engine," said Roy. "Can it?" he demanded.

"No. No, of course not!" Geesel turned to Snag. "That," he barked, "is what you should have done! You see how simple it is when you use your head."

"But I didn't want these two tuh know there was a plot tuh ruin 'em," protested the killer. "Now they know beyond a doubt that you're plottin' ag'in them."

"And what of it? Can they prove it? Isn't it their word against mine?" Geesel quoted several things Roy had said, to show how utterly improbable it was that he should find himself in difficulties. He talked as much to convince himself as for any other reason.

"Pay me," said Roy.

Geesel drew out a bulging wallet, slipped off the wide rubber band that held it and counted bills into the cowboy's outstretched hand.

"Two hundred and fifty dollars," he growled, looking toward Snag. "And that's only part of it."

"There's seven hundred and fifty to come, isn't there, Geesel?" asked Roy.

Geesel nodded.

"A thousand dollars," howled Snag Pritchard. "Is that what you're puttin' out to that critter?"

"It is! And all because you were an incompetent bungler."

Dick Collins wanted to trust Roy, but it was becoming increasingly hard. He saw the money changing hands and thought bitterly how much that same amount of cash would have meant to him. With it he could have put the engine into working order, bought a new boiler if necessary. He could have hired men to carry on with Gimlet. He could, unquestionably, have brought in the oil with the cash Roy was being paid for destroying the engine.

Roy said, "On the first of the month you pay the balance, Geesel, then you'll be given back the letter of agreement. Is that clear?"

"It seems to me," replied Geesel, "you should call it square right now. The cash I've already given you is mighty big pay for what you've done."

Roy smiled and said, "We'll stick to our agreement, Geesel."

"All right," replied the moneylender with poor grace. He looked at the derrick, which hadn't been damaged by the blast. He looked at it as his own, and began roughly estimating the cost of resuming operations. The winch and windlass, cables, and most of the other equipment had remained intact. The engine alone had suffered from the blast. He felt that he'd made a shrewd investment in Roy Rogers, even at a thousand dollars. He looked at Roy and found a strange expression on the cowboy's face.

Roy glanced at his watch, then off toward the east. He saw a cloud of dust in the distance, and snapped his fingers in satisfaction.

"Right on time," he said. "It's swell of them."

"What are you talking about?" demanded Geesel.

"You," said Roy, "are due for the shock of your life."

"What?"

Roy turned to Dick Collins and Gimlet. He waved the bills he'd taken from Abe Geesel.

"Hold everything," he cried gaily. "The real fireworks are just about to start!"

CHAPTER TWENTY-SEVEN

Dick and Gimlet saw a number of horsemen, far off in the distance toward the east. It was impossible to tell how many there were. They were, as yet, too distant.

Gimlet could only stare when he saw the expression on Roy's face. The young cowboy looked at Geesel with loathing. Geesel seemed to know something was about to happen. He stared, open-mouthed, and fell back a couple of paces.

"Don't back away," snapped Roy. "I want to talk to you, Geesel. You've been playing a dirty game. In fact, it's just about the dirtiest game I've ever run up against."

"Wha-what's the matter with you?" faltered Geesel. "Y-You've got your money, haven't you?"

"I," said Roy, "have *your* money."

"W-Well I—I mean to say—"

"I'll do the talking," cut in Roy sharply. "You made an agreement with Dick Collins. You tied him up so he couldn't get cash to continue his work here unless you provided that cash. You did everything you could to block his success. You planned to let him and his partners do most of the work here, then

235

move out while you stepped in and took up an option they weren't supposed to know about."

"Now see here, why're you going through all this?" asked Abe Geesel.

"Because I'm going to use your money to bring in this oil well!"

Geesel stared at the speaker. His jaw fell open and for a moment he was speechless.

Roy Rogers went on, "Do you understand me, Geesel? I'm using *your own money*, just as your agreement with Collins demands. Now you'd better get set for a few more shocks, Geesel, because they're coming!"

Roy's hand shot forward. Before Geesel could fall back, the cowboy had snatched a small pistol from a holster beneath the rusty-looking coat.

"You won't need this," he barked. "All you'll need is a few feet of strong rope."

Roy jerked a length of line from his pocket, and before Geesel could gather his dazed senses to put up a show of resistance, he found himself tossed to the ground with Roy sitting astride him, tying his hands together.

Gimlet and Dick could have let out whoops of applause, as they saw the man they hated being tied so quickly and efficiently.

Back on his feet, Roy pulled his knife and cut the ropes that held Dick and Gimlet. "The stage setting

"You'd Better Get Set, Geesel. Here They Come."

can be taken away," he grinned.

"What in tarnation are you goin' to do next?" howled Gimlet. "First you make us think we're the ones that are gettin' the short end of the stick, then it turns out that you was on our side all the time. Now what?"

"Stick around, Gimlet. The best is yet to come."

Geesel was beside himself. He bellowed at Snag, but found scant sympathy there.

"Yuh thought you was gettin' a fine deal from Rogers," the killer sneered. "Thought he was doin' such a slick job an' that I was such a bungler! Wal, you're gettin' what you asked for, yuh mangy old miser!"

The oncoming horsemen could be recognized. Gimlet saw Jim Lambert, the sheriff, at the head of the group, with a couple of deputies close behind him. There were others, obscured by the clouds of dust.

"The sheriff!" yelled Gimlet. "Doggone it all, Dick, thar's the sheriff comin' full speed!"

"Look who's behind him," said Roy.

"Deputies."

"Behind the deputies."

Dick managed to prop himself on his uninjured side to watch the horsemen. A long-legged, rangy man rode into view behind the sheriff.

Gimlet fairly screamed. "It's Steve! Steve Logan!

My old pal! The best friend I ever had! What's he comin' here for?"

"Can't you guess?" asked Roy.

Gimlet shook his head.

"I telephoned him last night, Gimlet, and told him you needed some help on this job."

"Y-Y-Yuh mean he—he's a-comin' tuh help us?"

"Sure he is."

"But hold on," said Dick. "We can't take his help—the agreement with Geesel—"

"Geesel is paying the bill, Dick. Don't worry! There'll be no violation of the contract."

"Look!" shouted Gimlet. "Look who else is comin'! Thar's Slim Anderson an' Barney Diggs! An' thar's Hank Foster an' Gimp Mullen! I know every mother's son o' them. Dick, Dick, doggone it, those critters are the best oil men in the hull doggoned world! Why, they c'n git oil from a hunk of concrete!"

"They're bringing a couple of wagons, Gimlet," Roy explained. "They know you need a new engine and some drills and a few other things to finish this job in jig time."

"An' they're bringin' all that stuff with 'em?"

"Sure they are. No use making an extra trip. They'll have some tents and food, too, because they plan to stay here until you've got your oil."

Salt tears filled Gimlet's only eye. This was almost

more than the old man's emotions could take. His friends, friends for many years, were rallying around him now to make a whirlwind finish of his project.

Dust swirled in great clouds as the riders reined up near the derrick. Gimlet was in the center of a laughing, shouting crowd of enthusiastic men. Several wagons clattered to the scene and strong arms started throwing out tents, bedding, huge supplies of food and cooking utensils. From another wagon, men lifted the parts of a used but serviceable engine.

"We brought one from my number three well," Steve Logan explained. "It's a darn fine little engine, too!"

Drills followed—a plentiful supply of them, all brand new and sharp.

Five men were on the platform assembling the engine. Two others were screwing a new drill into the bit. Gears were being oiled, new cables installed.

Steve Logan's men were well trained. They knew what they were doing. They were going after oil and they knew how to get it. No longer would there be any compromise with makeshift equipment, dull tools and faulty machinery. Steve Logan had brought the best of everything that could possibly be needed, including a plentiful supply of high-powered explosive. He'd also brought manpower enough to operate three shifts in twenty-four hours. There were gasoline lights to furnish illumination for work at night.

Steve and Gimlet were side by side watching the men unload.

"This is goin' to be fun," said Steve. "Many a time the two of us have brought in a well, eh, Gimlet?"

"You bet," the old man agreed.

"Remember how we used to say that some day we'd bring in a well for ourselves?"

"You got yours all right, Steve. I was mighty glad about that."

"Wal, now it's yore turn, Gimlet!"

During all the excitement, Geesel and Snag writhed in their ropes. Geesel maintained a steady demand for the attention of Jim Lambert, who was engaged in a low-voiced conversation with Roy. Finally he went to the moneylender.

"What do you want, Geesel?" he asked.

"Untie me. Get these ropes off. I demand my release."

"No hurry about that," replied the sheriff coolly.

"This can't go on! Those men can't work here! They can't furnish equipment to Collins and Lonergan!"

"Why not?"

"It violates our contract. I know my rights. I know the law. I—"

"Just a minute," said Roy, stepping forward.

"You keep out of this!" fumed Geesel.

"Your agreement says you've got to furnish the cash for this job. Isn't that right?"

"You know it is."

"You heard him admit that, Sheriff?"

The official nodded.

Roy held out a handful of bills. "Here," he said, "are two hundred and fifty dollars that Geesel gave me a little while ago." He turned to Geesel and said, "Why did you give me this money, Geesel?"

The miser stared at the bills. He looked at Jim Lambert, then at Roy.

"What's the matter?" asked Roy. "Why don't you answer the question? Why did you give me this cash?"

Geesel fumbled with syllables without saying anything.

"I have a paper in my pocket, Geesel, proving that you gave it to me. You remember signing that paper, don't you?"

"Uh—er—uh—ugh—"

"I think anyone could identify your signature," Roy went on mercilessly. "I can show the sheriff the agreement you signed, if I have to, but I don't think that will be necessary. You can simply tell him and his deputies that you handed the cash to me, to use for hiring men and renting equipment."

Geesel felt as if the world were falling on his head. He was overcome by the perfection of the trap into which he had fallen. If Roy produced the incriminating paper, he would be doomed. He'd have no part of the oil well after the trick that document would prove. The truth would jail him. He heard Roy's voice again.

"Of course," Roy said smoothly, "two hundred and fifty dollars won't cover the expenses, but Geesel agreed to pay another seven hundred and fifty dollars on the first of the month. That, I think, will cover everything. Logan's bill won't be any more than that."

"Well?" snapped the sheriff. "What about it, Geesel? Is that true? Did you agree to pay a thousand dollars so the well could be brought in?"

"I—I d-don't know I—" Geesel was still groping for words.

"Never mind answering," said Roy, reaching into his pocket. "I can show the sheriff your signature."

"That isn't necessary!" exclaimed Abe Geesel quickly. "I—I'm paying the bill," he moaned.

"Then Collins is not violating his agreement with you?"

Geesel could only shake his head.

CHAPTER TWENTY-EIGHT

THE OUTCOME

"Now that you have Geesel's admission that Dick Collins is well within the terms of his agreement, there are a few other things to clear up," said Roy to the sheriff.

Jim Lambert nodded. "Some murders," he said.

"I guess there's no doubt about who killed Dick's brother."

"Indian Pete. He paid for that," the sheriff said. "That was Indian Pete's job."

"But someone incited Indian Pete!"

"I think you're right about that," agreed the sheriff.

Snag's eyes were wide and staring. He hadn't been particularly concerned with Abe Geesel's difficult spot. In fact, he had rather enjoyed seeing the tight-fisted schemer squirm. Now the conversation between the sheriff and Roy Rogers was on unpleasant ground.

"The three half-breeds who were with Indian Pete could have named the man causing the trouble. That's why they were killed," Roy said.

"Who was it?" asked the sheriff.

Roy turned toward Snag Pritchard.

"There," he said, "is the killer! I think you'll find Abe Geesel more than willing to place all the blame on Pritchard. One of these two will turn State's evidence to save himself from the hangman's rope.

"Of course," Roy continued, "Snag didn't commit murder for nothing. He was hired for the job. Abe Geesel hired him!"

"That's a lie!" screamed Geesel. "It's not true! You can't frame me for those murders!"

"Do you," demanded Roy, "mean to say you wouldn't hire someone to keep my friends from getting their oil out of this ground?"

"Why should I do that? Why should I, when I own a quarter interest in it?" Geesel turned to the sheriff and said, "I'm as much interested in seeing oil brought in here as Dick Collins is!"

"Oh, no, you're not! You had John Clayton take out a second option on this land in his name. But *you* own that option. You wanted Dick to lose the land so you could buy it. You wanted *all* of this property, instead of a quarter of it!"

"No! No! No!" Geesel howled. "You can't believe that, Sheriff. He can't prove it."

"Oh, yes, I can," snapped Roy. He whipped the signed agreement from his pocket. "You hired Snag to incite Indian Pete! You hired Snag to kill the half-breeds. You hired him to block this job. And, when he failed, you hired *me!*" Roy thrust the agreement into Jim Lambert's hand. "There's the proof!" he said. "There's what Geesel offered me to stop work on this job!"

Jim Lambert scanned the paper. He'd already read it through the night before.

"I guess this'll do to start with," he said to Geesel. "Maybe, when you and Pritchard get squealin' on each other, a lot of the truth will come out."

Geesel tried to argue. "Wait a minute," he said. "You see that agreement! If Rogers got the cash because of that agreement it stands to reason he didn't get it to finance this job!"

"What are you talking about, Geesel?"

"I *did* give him some cash," Geesel went on desperately. "I did hand him two hundred and fifty dollars, just as that agreement says, and it wasn't to pay for bringing in oil. That money wasn't for Dick Collins! See here, Lambert, if you're going to claim I paid Rogers to block this job, then Collins can't use the cash!"

Roy smiled at Geesel. "Geesel," he said, "you're all wrong! You stated in front of witnesses that you provided the money for the job!"

"But according to that paper—"

"According to the paper you're to pay me a specified sum after you've seen me *prevent* the completion of the oil well. How can you say you've seen me prevent anything, when I'm the one who phoned for all these men to come and finish the job?"

Geesel tried to salvage something from the ruins of his plans. "Well, if you don't block it, I don't have to pay another seven-fifty on the first of the month."

"To me?" asked Roy. "No, of course not. You don't owe me a dime, because I haven't done what you wanted me to do."

Geesel nodded.

"But," added Roy, "you said, in the presence of the sheriff and his deputies, that you'd pay for Steve Logan's work. That was a verbal agreement, Geesel, and you'll be held to it."

"By that time, money won't mean much to you, anyhow," put in the sheriff. "You'll be waitin' for the sentence of the court to be carried out."

Weeks later Roy Rogers sat in the bunkhouse of the X-Bax-X Ranch. He had had his fill of the oil game and had decided that the life of a cowboy was the life for him.

He was reading a clipping from the Gopher Creek newspaper, which Dick Collins had sent to him. It told how evidence had been introduced at the trial of Abe Geesel and Snag Pritchard. The evidence consisted of receipts for money paid by the money-lender. The receipts had been signed by Snag Pritchard and the money had been paid to him— for murder.

The door opened and a cowboy handed Roy a large box, tightly tied and crudely addressed. It was postmarked, "Gopher Creek."

"The mail's here. This box came fer you," the cowboy said.

Roy pulled a knife from its sheath on his belt and cut the cords. Lifting the cover, he found a single sheet of paper over a soggy mass wrapped in water-proof paper. A reek of raw oil rose from the package. Roy read the note. It was short and to the point.

"They hung Snag and Geesel this morning," the note said. "I thought you'd like my old clothes for a souvenir. As you can see, I sure had my bath in oil when the well came in. I plumb wallered in it, and it was swell." The note was signed, "Yore friend, Gimlet."

There was a short postscript: "P.S. The sheriff gave me back my gun."

WHITMAN
AUTHORIZED EDITIONS

NEW STORIES OF ADVENTURE
AND MYSTERY

Up-to-the-minute novels for boys and girls about Favorite Characters, all popular and well-known, including—

INVISIBLE SCARLET O'NEIL

LITTLE ORPHAN ANNIE and the Gila Monster Gang

BRENDA STARR, Girl Reporter

DICK TRACY, Ace Detective

DICK TRACY Meets the Night Crawler

TILLIE THE TOILER and the Masquerading Duchess

BLONDIE and Dagwood's Adventure in Magic

BLONDIE and Dagwood's Snapshot Clue

TOM HARMON and the Great Gridiron Plot

BETTY GRABLE and the House With the Iron Shutters

BOOTS (of "Boots and Her Buddies") and the Mystery of the Unlucky Vase

THE SON OF THE PHANTOM

JUDY GARLAND and the Hoodoo Costume

JANE WITHERS and the Swamp Wizard

BLUE STREAK and Doctor Medusa

WHITMAN
AUTHORIZED EDITIONS